Blue Hydrangeas

Praise for Blue Hydrangeas

"The author covered some of the most difficult situations families are dealing with, and I can see our caregivers connecting to the husband and son." - Meg E. Boyce, LMSW, Vice President Programs and Services Alzheimer's Association, Poughkeepsie, NY

"Marianne Sciucco not only did a wonderful job writing a beautiful novel about a couple experiencing dementia, but did it in a thoughtful, authentic, humane way." Donna Davies, LCSW, Alzheimer's Association, Hudson Valley/Rockland/Westchester, NY Chapter

'Blue Hydrangeas traces a couple's struggle with Alzheimer's in an effective story that doesn't pull its punches, but remains compassionate and absorbing." - Liz Lynch for IndieReader

"*Blue Hydrangeas* is, by far, the most tender love story I've read in a very long time. While not a 'happily ever after' love story, Blue Hydrangeas is sure to be one you will ponder for some time after you have finished reading it." - Lee Ambrose for *Story Circle Book Reviews*

"Marianne Sciucco has written a charming love story dealing with real life happiness and tragedy. Sara and Jack could be the story of my grandparents, my parents, and my own future reality. I felt their pain and shared in their joys. I absolutely loved this book and give it a ten star rating." - Trudi LoPreto for Readers' Favorite

"While reading Marianne Sciucco's fictional story I was taken back to the years of caretaking and decision-making for my own parents who both died of Alzheimer's disease. Thank you, Marianne, for writing a beautiful love story portraying the honest devastation of the disease, yet reinforcing the desire to preserve the dignity of those afflicted." – Jean L. Lee, author of *Alzheimer's Daughter*

"*Blue Hydrangeas is a tender love story, describing the plight of an older couple grappling with aging and its foibles. The wife in this novel has descended into the rabbit hole of dementia and her husband is doing his very best to honor his commitment to stand by her side, at any cost, to the point of near disaster. If you've ever had a loved one with dementia, you'll find this poignant story rings quite true to the challenges, heartbreak, and turbulent emotions that often go hand-in-hand with this devastating disease.*" – *Vicki Tapia, author of* Somebody Stole My Iron, a Family History of Dementia

"What a touching account of a couple's journey into Alzheimer's and of the love that never succumbed to the disease! Marianne Sciucco captured all the levels of feelings and fears that accompany this journey – the doubting, the rationalization that everything is ok, the hoping... and finally the acceptance. Most of all, she captured the love that so often brings out strengths that will help caregivers and their loved ones as they face this together. A truly remarkable story!" – Marilynn Garzione, author of *Released to the Angels: Discovering the Hidden Gifts of Alzheimer's*

"*My own mom has suffered for over nine years from Alzheimer's, so as a caregiver myself, I understand what a family lives with. After reading the author's bio, I see that she is a nurse and that this was not a story involving her own personal family. Marianne was able to describe and capture the feelings that this family was going through, as if it was her own family's tragedy. Bravo for a well written book that captivated me as I* read each page." - *Lisa Hirsch -author of* My Mom My Hero.

"This book is my story too. I was my mother's caregiver for over 4 years, and now I'm the caregiver for her widower husband. This book just showed up in front of my eyes one day when I needed it so much yet didn't realize it. As I began reading I could tell why I felt the story reach deeply into a part of me that nothing else had even come close to touching. Instead of thinking Jack had many of the same challenges that I have, I felt that I am the one who is somewhat like Jack, only I could clearly see how I needed to correct my attitude. May the Good Lord grace me with the compassion, patience and unconditional love I can so clearly see in Jack, and in those who support him. What a beautiful book. Thank you." - S. D. Murphy

"This book is a MUST to read. As a gerontologist, I truly appreciated all of the topics that were covered in the book. The sensitive subjects of caregiving, progression of the disease were accurately and expertly woven into the story. Alzheimer's disease not only affects the stricken individual, but the family unit as well. The author does a fabulous and in depth job of depicting the powerful emotions of the characters. I simply could not put this book down." - Susan J. Hurt

"I read this book almost straight through. What a great storyline and so very accurate in the portrayal of the devastation the disease takes on its victims. The author also shows the great love and sacrifice of the spouse for those fewer and fewer moments of clarity. A great read whether you have the disease in the family or not. What a love story!" - Cynthia Hoelscher

"Reading this lovely book has been a gift indeed. - M.J. Sherman

Blue Hydrangeas

Marianne Sciucco

(pronounced shoo-koh)

Bunky Press

Published by Bunky Press
Copyright © 2013 by Marianne Sciucco
All Rights Reserved

The persons and events portrayed in this work of fiction are the creations of the author. Any resemblance to persons living or dead is purely coincidental.

978-0-9895592-0-1

Cover by Perry Elisabeth Design
perryelisabethdesign.blogspot.com

Images © piyato, 4774344sean | canstockphoto.com

Bunky Press artwork © patrimonio designs ltd/ shutterstock

Author Photo © Lou Sciucco

I dedicate this book to the millions
of people who are living with or have
lived with Alzheimer's disease,
their loved ones, and their caregivers.
Special dedication is to my aunts:
Gilda Cioto Grasso,
Stella Kasica Vassell,
Lorraine Kacy Kasica,
and to my husband's grandmother,
Laura Duvoli Salamone.
Rest in peace, gentle women.

Prologue

While night settled on Blue Hydrangeas, Jack and Sara lay nestled on the couch, wrapped in a hand-knit afghan, and clinging to each other as silent as stones.

The lights were out, a crackling fire lit the room, and shadows danced on the walls. He cradled her in his arms and stared into space, detached. She focused on the fire, unyielding in his embrace, so far away. The Bach he had put on the CD player had long ended. Outside, the first snowfall of winter blanketed Cape Cod.

He had done all he could to make this evening the same as any other, but this godawful quiet made everything seem so wrong. After forty-five years of marriage, it wouldn't have surprised him if they had run out of things to say, but not a day ended without some new insight or tidbit of information passing between them. They shared everything—their deepest fears, their most private thoughts. Tonight, there was nothing, just this palpable silence, as they ruminated separately on their visit to Dr. Fallon and the horrifying news he had given them.

Jack pondered the same troublesome thoughts over and over, making no progress in absorbing the doctor's diagnosis. He knew enough about Alzheimer's to fill him with fear, a fear he had not experienced since his days as a medic in World War II. Back then he had lived in anticipation of the next strike, the next slew of injured and casualties. He could not sleep. He could not eat. Uncertainty consumed every moment. Sara's Alzheimer's filled him with the same fear and anxiety. He did not know what to expect, or when, or how bad it would be.

Some situations defy words, and there were no words, no phony reassurances, to make this right. If there were, he could not pretend to know them.

The room grew dark as the fire burned low. The logs he had stoked an hour before were turning to ash. Neither of them had the drive or the energy to get up and throw on another log.

At last, she broke through the mournful silence. "I'm going to lose everything," she said, her voice a hoary whisper, a voice he had never heard before.

"Don't say that," he started, but she interrupted.

"Whatever happens," she said, "stay with me. I can't bear to suffer through this without you." A single tear rolled down her cheek.

"Sh," Jack whispered. He brushed away the tear, and made a promise only prayer would help him keep. "Nothing like that is going to happen. I'll never leave you. We're staying right here." He pulled the afghan tighter around them, sealing out the chill that slowly descended on the room as the fire waned.

They sat in silence for a long time, long enough for the fire to go out, and then he helped her off the couch and took her to bed.

Nine years later...

Chapter One

Jack closed his eyes in frustration and counted to ten.

Sara had emerged from the bedroom in an outfit made for raking autumn leaves. A knitted cap that had seen better days sat lopsided over her uncombed hair. She wore one of his old sweaters, frayed at the wrists and coming apart under one arm. She clomped through the house in a heavy pair of work boots. Where did she find these ridiculous garments? He thought he'd sent that sweater to the Goodwill long ago.

He glanced at the clock and sighed with exasperation. They had errands to run: the pharmacy, the post office, the market. "Come on, Sara. I can't take you out dressed like that," he said.

"What's wrong with it? This sweater will keep me warm, and these boots are good for walking."

"It's summer, that's what's wrong with it. Today's a scorcher. It's eighty degrees and only half-past nine. Put on a pair of shorts and a blouse and let's go." He reached for her cap. "And get rid of this."

She blocked his arm, grabbed the other, and gave him a nasty pinch. "I can't go anywhere without my cap," she cried, darting away.

Jack yelped in pain. Clutching his aching forearm, he chased after her through the dining room, the kitchen, the living room, and back again, before facing off at the single step leading into the family room. Again, he reached for the cap. She lunged forward to deliver another pinch and they lost their balance, falling over the step. Sara landed on her right hip with a terrific bang. Jack landed on top of her.

That's it, he thought, afraid she'd broken a leg, hip, or worse. He pulled himself upright, groaning as his stiff joints protested. He tried to stand her, a tiny, wiry woman, but she felt like dead weight and resisted his efforts, howling like a wounded dog. He bent over her, and with his strong but gentle hands grasped her right leg and cautiously checked its range of motion.

She clawed at him and screamed, "Let go of me, you old fool, I've hurt my leg."

18

He removed his hands and tried to stand up but she pulled him back down on to the floor.

"I've hurt my leg," she cried. "I can't get up."

"I know," he grunted, breathless from his exertions. "I'm trying to help you."

She wouldn't let him go, but he needed to call for help. He struggled to pull himself free and wrenched his own back, sending a violent spasm up from his lower spine to between his shoulders.

"Good God," he cried, and she released him.

He staggered to the phone and called the paramedics. Then he dropped down on the floor beside her and spoke to her with soothing words.

"It's all right," he said. "Everything's going to be all right." He stroked her face, her hair, and repeated this mantra until she settled down. When she had quieted, he reached into his pocket, pulled out a tiny vial of medicine, and placed a little pill under his tongue to quell the ache in his chest.

Jack felt wiped out, unable to go on. Their day-to-day battle with Sara's dementia exhausted him. It was a relentless battle of small hopeful gains alternating with frequent devastating losses. Just that morning, she'd awakened at three and slipped out of bed without making a sound. The clatter of pots and pans in the dead of night dragged him out of a deep sleep, and he stumbled into the kitchen to find her hard at work brewing pots of coffee and baking blueberry muffins.

Years ago, it would not have been unusual. They had operated their home, Blue Hydrangeas, as a bed and breakfast for almost a decade, but Sara had forgotten they'd closed for business a few summers back.

Jack played along with her frequent lapses in memory to maintain peace in their home. It was demanding, discouraging work, and at the end of some days he felt ready to give up. But, when morning came things always seemed better and he gave each new day another go. The days rolled into weeks, months, and then years, and here they were, together at home, just the two of them with Sara's Alzheimer's.

He knew it was important to keep her in the present, but in the middle of the night he didn't have the energy. She ignored his desperate pleas to go back to bed, insisting she had work to do. Wary of starting an argument, he poured himself a cup of strong coffee and waited for the muffins to bake. When no guests came down for breakfast, her disappointment broke his heart.

Jack heard the ambulance pull into the driveway and extricated himself from Sara's grasp.

"Where are you going?" she asked. "Don't leave me here lying on the floor."

"Hold on, Sara," he said. "Help is on the way."

He limped to the door and greeted the paramedics.

"I'm sorry to call you out like this," he said, "but my wife has fallen again and I can't lift her."

"No problem, Mr. Harmon," said the first paramedic, a young man named Robert whom Jack recognized from a previous emergency call to the house. "We'll take care of her."

Jack led them to the family room where Sara still lay sprawled on the step. She looked at the men warily and asked, "Who are you?"

"Hello, Sara," Robert said. "I heard you had a fall."

"I can't get up," she said. "It's all his fault." She pointed at Jack.

"Now, Sara," Jack said, "it was an accident."

"Accident, schmaccident," she said. "It's all your fault."

"Can you tell me what happened, Mr. Harmon?" Robert asked as he knelt beside Sara.

"It was a silly thing," Jack explained. "A silly argument over her cap."

"He won't let me wear my cap," Sara said. "Ouch!" she cried as Robert and his partner Jeremy tried to reposition her.

"It's okay," Sara," said Robert. "I just need to examine you and make sure nothing's broken."

"Get your hands off me!" she shrieked. "You're hurting me." She slapped at their hands. "Let me go or I'm calling the police."

"Now, there's no need for that," Jeremy said. "We're done here. We're taking you to the hospital to get you checked out."

"The hospital? I don't want to go to the hospital."

"You need to go, Sara," Jack said. "You may have broken your leg."

"Probably not, Mr. Harmon," said Robert as he and Jeremy rose, "but we need to make sure. I'm going to take your blood pressure, Sara, while my buddy here goes out to get the stretcher. Is that okay?"

Sara watched him pull out a stethoscope and blood pressure cuff. "Don't break my arm," she said.

"Of course not," said Robert. He did a quick assessment of her vitals. "Blood pressure's a little low," he told Jack, "but pulse is steady."

"Thank God," said Jack. He hovered over Sara. "Is there much pain?" he asked her.

"Of course there's pain," she said. "What a silly question."

Jeremy arrived with the stretcher and the paramedics lifted Sara to place her on it.

"Go easy, go easy," she said, grimacing.

"Please don't hurt her," Jack said.

"We're trying not to," said Jeremy, "but she may be uncomfortable while we move her."

"Oh," Sara cried, "stop! Stop it I say, you're killing me." She swatted at them, making it difficult to complete the transfer without jostling her. "Put me down," she ordered.

"We're all done," said Robert as he covered her with a sheet and strapped her in. They began rolling the stretcher toward the front door. Jack followed, limping and massaging his lower back.

"Are you okay, Mr. Harmon?" asked Robert. "You look like you're in pain."

"I'm all right," Jack said. "Just a twinge in my back."

"He fell, too," said Sara, "right on top of me."

"Whoa, wait a minute," said Robert, stopping at the door. "Let me check you out."

Jack shook his head. "I'm fine. I'm more worried about Sara. Let's get her to the hospital. I'll get checked out once I know she's okay."

They exited the house and proceeded to the ambulance. Once Sara was secured in the back with an attentive Robert at her side, Jack climbed into the passenger seat up front with Jeremy who whisked them away to the hospital.

A few hours later, the doctor released Jack from the ER. X-rays of his back had turned out fine. An electrocardiogram revealed no new changes. His blood pressure was way up, but after a dose of intravenous medication it returned to a safe level. The ER doctor told him to follow-up with his primary care physician in the morning, prescribed muscle relaxants for his back pain, and advised him to take it easy.

Sara was not so lucky. Her right hip and leg were intact, but she had suffered severe

Marianne Sciucco

bruising and the leg was swollen and tender. It was difficult for her to bear weight. The doctor also discovered she had a serious urinary tract infection and was dehydrated. He admitted her to the hospital for a few days of intravenous antibiotics and fluids. In the morning, she'd start physical therapy.

Jack went along with the nurses and orderlies to help settle Sara in her room. When they left, he moved a chair over to the side of the bed, and waited while she pulled up the covers and shifted around trying to get comfortable. After she stopped fidgeting, he held a cup of cranberry juice to her parched lips and offered her the straw.

"What are we doing now?" she asked, her voice cranky with exhaustion.

"We're going to have lunch," he said. It was well after noon.

"Here?" she asked, before taking a long sip of juice.

"Yes."

"What is this place?"

"It's the hospital, Sara. We've been here before." Her long snowy hair matched the pure white of the linens. He finger-combed the tangled mess, trying to make her look more like herself. At home, he brushed it every night, one hundred strokes, until it shone like silk.

She nodded and sucked down the last of the juice. Jack placed the empty cup on the table.

"Are we staying here all day?"

24

"You're staying here. I'm going home."

"I don't want to stay here. I want to go home with you."

Jack squeezed her hand. "Maybe tomorrow."

"Why do I have to stay?" Her eyes turned dark, the way they did when she was gearing up for a fight.

"Because Dr. Fallon wants you to stay," he said in his don't-argue-with-me tone. "You need medicine, Sara."

"I have medicine at home."

"Not this kind of medicine." He pointed to the intravenous tubing and bags of fluids and antibiotics hanging on the tall metal pole next to her bed.

"I don't see what all the fuss is about," she said, plucking at the sheets. "I feel fine."

A cheerful nursing assistant entered the room, providing a welcome distraction. "Hello, Mrs. Harmon," she said. "Back with us again?" Jack recognized Verlaine, his favorite nursing assistant on the hospital's staff. She carried a food tray and placed it on the overbed table within Sara's reach.

"What have we here?" Verlaine asked, opening the containers of food. "Chicken, white rice, and steamed carrots." She cut the chicken and vegetables into bite-sized pieces. "And you've got milk and a bowl of chocolate pudding." She spread a napkin over Sara's chest and boosted the head of the bed up so

Marianne Sciucco

she could reach her food. "Anything else I can get you?" she asked with a beautiful smile.

"No, thanks," Jack said. Sara had started eating, seeming to have forgotten he and Verlaine were still in the room.

"Take care, Mr. Harmon," Verlaine called as she left them alone.

Jack watched Sara eat. Dr. Fallon had made it clear that a proper diet was important to maintain Sara's stability, and Jack took meal times seriously. She had a good appetite, although sometimes he had to prod her into eating anything at all. She often left meals unfinished and sometimes hid unwanted food behind the couch or at the back of a kitchen cabinet where it turned bad before Jack found it. However, for this meal Sara was settled in and eating happily. His own stomach rumbled, reminding him he had not eaten since the blueberry muffins earlier that morning. He'd also missed his noon medications.

"Honey, I'm going down to the cafeteria to get some lunch."

Sara was concentrating on her pudding and did not look up.

At the elevator, her case manager, Allison, approached him. Her job was to assist patients and their families with arranging the aftercare that followed a hospitalization.

"Mr. Harmon, I'm glad I ran into you," she said, all business. "We need to talk." She was a strapping woman, mid-forties, with a kind face and a no-nonsense attitude.

"It's a beautiful day, Allison. You should sneak out and take a walk," Jack said, sidestepping her. "I won't tell," he winked. The elevator doors opened and he moved forward.

Allison refused to let him get away. She took him by the arm and led him into her office. "Has anything changed at home since your wife's hospital visit last month?" she asked.

"Oh, no," he explained, smiling. "My grandson Derek is still staying with us."

Allison said, "Your grandson works full-time."

"Well, yes, of course," Jack said, "but he helps out when he's home. I also have Mrs. Wright, my housekeeper, coming in every morning, and Margie, Sara's companion, is available whenever I need her. Then there's our good friend, Rose Fantagucci, just down the road, and you know my son and his wife are a short ride away up in Boston. I've got it all covered."

The case manager frowned. "That's not enough, Mr. Harmon. Your wife needs dependable twenty-four hour care."

"But I'm there twenty-four hours. I never leave her alone."

Allison sighed. "Full-time caregiving is a tough job. We've talked about this before. It's time, Mr. Harmon. This is too much for you. Sara should be in a place where her needs are met twenty-four seven. One person can't possibly fulfill that responsibility." During Sara's many hospitalizations the case managers and nurses had questioned Jack's ability to care for his wife. Today it was Allison's turn to convince him that an alternative living arrangement was in Sara's best interest.

"You mean a nursing home," Jack said, gagging on the words. The thought sickened him. So many of those afflicted with Alzheimer's finished their days in nursing homes, and he was determined to keep Sara with him for as long as possible. Forever. He'd never consent to an arrangement that would take her from Blue Hydrangeas.

"Not a nursing home, Mr. Harmon," Allison explained, "but an assisted living facility, where Sara will receive around-the-clock supervision by people trained to meet her special needs. Think of it as a bridge between living at home and living in a nursing home."

"You're not fooling me," he said. "It's the same thing. Either way, we'll be separated, and I promised Sara we'd stay together in our home no matter what."

"You might consider assisted living for yourself as well, Mr. Harmon, given your heart condition—"

Jack wouldn't let her finish. "This is nuts," he said. "I'm perfectly capable of caring for Sara on my own. I love my wife. Don't worry about us, Allison. We'll be all right." He patted the case manager's arm.

"Mr. Harmon, this isn't about love," she said. "It's about your wife's care and safety. Love is not enough."

"You're very kind, Allison, and I appreciate your concern, but I'll let you know when I've had enough. Right now, I need to get some lunch." He walked out of her office.

After dining on the cafeteria's daily special he returned to his wife, now sleeping peacefully, her face devoid of any stress. Jack stared at her for a long while, seeing vestiges of a young Sara, remembering the first time he had seen her fifty-seven years ago. Sara was nineteen, a blue-eyed beauty with rich auburn hair and tiny freckles splashed across her tiny nose. The face he saw now was older and well seasoned, but at seventy-six she was still a beauty.

The auburn hair had turned snow white and covered her shoulders like a silken shawl. Her blue eyes still sparkled like jewels, but now tiny lines framed them. He smiled, thinking of how she lamented those wrinkles, blaming herself, a redhead living her life in the sun. She had taken care, but her love for the outdoors, the ocean, and her gardens had gotten the better of her. Jack thought the wrinkles added character, a testament to a life well lived.

Her hands, though, revealed the most about her. Once as soft as rose petals, they had become calloused and worn by her life's work.

As a commercial artist, she had dipped them into oil paint and turpentine for decades. And, when her hands were not commanding a paintbrush they had dug deep into the earth, creating a spectacular garden that reaped awards from gardening groups throughout New England.

Jack loved those hands, and held both of them in his own. Over the years, he had lavished her with exquisite jewelry, but these days she wore one simple gold band on her wedding finger, delicately inscribed with the words: "Always, my love. Jack." He stroked the ring, gazing at her with a mixture of love and grief. The last nine years had been tough and promised to get tougher. He sensed change, and loss, and death ahead and it filled him with fear deeper than he had ever known. The realization that one of them would die, would leave the other, paralyzed him. How could he live without her? What would she do without him?

"Oh, Sara," he whispered, a catch in his throat. Tears formed in his eyes and he brushed them away. He did not know whom he pitied more: Sara or himself.

He pulled away from her bedside and went home to call their son.

Chapter Two

Blue Hydrangeas was a stately colonial sprawled across two airy acres in Falmouthport,
Massachusetts, a picturesque Cape Cod village
perched on the edge of Nantucket Sound. It
was Jack and Sara's dream house and they'd
named it in honor of the beautiful flowering
bushes she adored and cultivated.

Jack entered through a side door adjacent to
the kitchen. The silence was painful; not even a
muffled television or radio program marred the
stillness. He tossed his keys on to the kitchen
counter, poured himself a glass of ice water,
and picked up the phone.

After Jack told him his mother was in the
hospital, his son, David, said, "Again? She was
in five times last year and four the year before,

not counting the trips to the emergency room. She's either dehydrated, or has a urinary tract infection, or some respiratory bug. Last month it was another fall. We have to do something about this, Dad. We need to come up with a better plan."

"What do you mean?" Jack asked, ever on guard. "Your mother's all right. These kinds of things happen to people our age. It's normal."

"No, Dad," David began, "it's not 'normal' for people your age to be in and out of the hospital. It's the Alzheimer's. The situation is out of control. Mom can't manage her own needs, and you can't manage yours *and* hers. She needs to go into some kind of nursing facility where she'll have plenty of people to care for her."

"Forget about it," Jack replied. "I can take care of her. I've taken care of her for years."

"Listen, Dad, the way it's going this disease will kill you first," David said. "You work night and day to care for Mom, but it's a tough job, and you don't let me help you." David and his wife had offered many times to stay with Sara so Jack could have some respite, but his father declined their offers, claiming he didn't want to interfere with their lives. David and Anne were college professors in Boston and had two college-age sons.

"You? What will you do? You have your own family, your own problems." Jack spoke with bitterness. "What is it with you young people, anyway? You're so eager to just give up and get out when things don't go your way. What happened to 'for better or for worse?' Don't people believe in marriage vows anymore?"

David sighed, and said, "I'm not asking you to break your marriage vows. I'm just saying Mom needs more help than you alone can provide."

Jack bristled. "I'm doing the best I can," he said. "You don't know what it's like to watch the woman you love disappear in front of your eyes. Sometimes I look at your mother and it's as if she's a stranger. I've lost her, and it breaks my heart." His voice wavered. "Other times, she makes me crazy. Yesterday, she turned on the water to fill the bathtub and forgot all about it. The bathroom flooded and I spent an hour cleaning it up." He stopped for a deep breath and David cut in.

"You see, Dad? You don't have enough hands or eyes to watch out for Mom."

"Anyway," Jack went on as though David had not spoken. "She still has good days, lots of them, and I won't give up on her. My family has never had anybody in an assisted living facility," oh, how he hated those words, "and I'm not going to be the first," he said, confident once David saw how well Sara looked after this brief hospitalization he'd drop this "facility" talk. No matter what he called it, the end was the same: Sara living among strangers in a strange place and him left alone in a big, empty house.

"Stubborn pride," David muttered.

Jack suffered from minor hearing loss, especially on the phone, but he heard his son's words and the frustration behind them. So many times these days he felt like he was the child and David the father. Before he could argue, David continued in a louder voice.

"Mom's safety is the most critical issue here," he said. "She's had several falls, and it's sheer luck she hasn't broken any bones. Who knows if the next one won't be catastrophic—a broken leg, or hip, or worse? What if she wanders away from the house and you can't find her? You live just a few blocks from the beach. What if she heads down there and goes for a swim? What if something happens to you and she forgets how to use the phone, forgets how to call 911?"

"David, you worry too much," Jack said.

"You bet I worry. I'm sorry, Dad, I hear what you're saying, but you have to admit things are getting worse by the week. I worry about your health. You have a bad heart, and this is very stressful."

"My heart is fine. I'm a healthy man, nothing wrong with me," Jack argued. Two heart attacks and a triple bypass had forced him into an early retirement from his career as a pharmaceuticals salesman, but he had felt fine for years.

"Dad, I'm well aware of your heart trouble. I don't need to lose two parents to this disease."

"I'm okay, David. Don't worry about me," Jack said with determination.

"And then there's the house," David went on, but Jack intercepted that old argument.

"Don't go there," he warned. "I have people to help with the house. There's no way I'm giving it up. This is your mother's house, her home."

"It's too much," David began, but Jack cut him off again.

"I know what I can handle," he said, his voice firm. "If it becomes too much for me, I'll let you know, but for now, nothing changes."

David knew when to call it quits. "I'm coming there tomorrow," he said. "I want to see Mom myself."

"It's not necessary," said his father, "but if you want to it's all right with me."

Three mornings later, as Jack made his way to Sara's hospital room, Allison, the case manager, pulled him aside.

"Good morning, Mr. Harmon. You'll be pleased to know I've completed the necessary paperwork and found a bed for your wife at several assisted living facilities in the area. If Dr. Fallon clears her for discharge she's ready to go today."

Jack stopped in his tracks. "You did what?" he asked, his voice rising. "Without my permission?"

Allison regarded him coolly. "It's well within my job duties," she explained.

Jack felt the familiar ache in his chest and fumbled in his pocket for the tiny vial of pills. He went to withdraw it, but then thought better of letting this woman see his discomfort. He left it where it was.

"Well, we'll just have to see what Dr. Fallon says about this," he said, moving away from her.

"Dr. Fallon knows all about it. He wrote the orders," Allison called after him.

Jack marched down the corridor toward Sara's room and bumped into a man in a long white lab coat.

"Jack," said a friendly voice. "What's your hurry?"

Jack pulled up short, recognizing Dr. Keith Fallon. He gave the physician an icy glare. "Did you write orders for Sara to go to some kind of a facility?"

The doctor avoided his eyes. "Yeah, Jack, I did." He glanced at his watch.

"Don't look at your watch, look at me. I told you I'd never send Sara to a nursing home or any kind of assisted living place. How dare you go behind my back and make these arrangements?"

He was making a scene. Visitors and patients stopped to stare. Hospital workers walked past, all ears. Other people's problems were a welcome distraction, and there was no better place to eavesdrop on people's troubles than in a hospital.

Sara's doctor pulled him into an empty room, away from the curious bystanders. "I'm sorry, Jack," he said. "Of course I would never be so presumptuous as to make arrangements without your knowledge. It's beyond my authority. I planned to call you before you got here but I had an emergency. I did ask the case manager to start looking for a facility for Sara."

Jack gaped at him. "Without speaking to me?" he sputtered.

"I know this seems sudden, and I understand your feelings, Jack, but I'm worried," Dr. Fallon said. "This last episode is over the top. You or Sara could have been seriously hurt this time. Your blood pressure was through the roof, and she doesn't seem to be thriving at home. We've been talking about this for months. I think it's time for some kind of nursing facility. Think about it, for your sake as well as for Sara's."

"Sorry, Doc," Jack said. "I gave her my word. No place but home. We'll manage."

Dr. Fallon fell silent and studied him from head to toe. "I know what you're thinking, Jack: a nursing facility is the last stop. But, I'm talking about an assisted living facility. Sure, there are nurses available, but it's more like a home for people who are having problems meeting their own needs because of illness."

"Sara has a home—with me. I take care of her needs," said Jack.

"You're right, Jack, you've been doing a wonderful job taking care of Sara, but lately things are spinning out of control. As the Alzheimer's advances, she needs more and more care and supervision. I know how hard you try, but one person simply can't manage it all. You need help around-the-clock to ease the load. "

"I'll get someone," Jack countered.

"You'd need several people to fill that need, and they're hard to find. That's why a facility is in her, and your, best interest. Everything will be managed for you, and you can see Sara as often as you want."

Jack was silent, deliberating these ideas. The thought of finding and hiring people he could trust with Sara's care, could trust in his home and depend upon to do their jobs, was daunting. Managing all of this on top of his other responsibilities was overwhelming.

Dr. Fallon went on. "How do you feel, Jack," he asked, "now that Sara's been in the hospital four days and you've had time for yourself, time to rest? You look great."

Jack paused for a moment to consider the doctor's words. When they had first come to the hospital he was at the end of his rope. It was a miracle they had not admitted him, too, what with his blood pressure being out of control and the angina acting up. These last few days at home without Sara had been peaceful. Free from constant worry and surveillance, he slept well and woke full of energy. He went to morning mass each day, something he missed because Sara's unpredictable outbursts made it difficult to bring her to church. After mass, he visited her at the hospital. He left at noon to have lunch and play cards with some old friends at his golf club, and for a few hours forgot his worries. At dinnertime, he went back to the hospital, picked up a meal in the cafeteria, and shared dinner with Sara. He stayed until visiting hours were over, and made it home in time to catch his favorite TV programs. The respite had done him good, although he'd never admit this to anyone, especially to Dr. Fallon. "I sleep well enough when she's home," he said.

"Honestly?" Dr. Fallon asked. "Don't forget: I'm your doctor, too. I bet if I checked your blood pressure right now it would be perfect."

Jack stared out the window at the clear July morning. He could not argue with Dr. Fallon. As part of his routine, he checked his blood pressure at home every day, and it had been perfect these last few days. And, there had been no angina; he had not taken any of the nitroglycerin pills since the day Sara went into the hospital.

Despair and confusion overwhelmed him. Maybe he *was* wrong, and Sara really did need others to help care for her. Maybe the time had finally come for him to step aside and let them take over. For nine years, he had been desperately clinging to the unraveling ends of a fragile rope, a rope that allowed Sara to remain in her own home, but he felt his grasp slipping. Her care was too extensive, too consuming for him to continue on his own, despite his hired help, his family, and his friends. He had done everything he could to stop this disease from destroying his wife, their marriage, their life together, but it was not possible. He was an old man with a damaged heart, and caring for Sara devoured every ounce of strength and energy he possessed.

Tentatively, he asked, "Do I get to choose the place?"

"Of course," the doctor said.

"What if she doesn't like it?"

"It's not a prison, Jack. Try it for a week. You can bring her home if either of you don't like it. We can always find another place."

A long minute passed while Jack considered this option. Finally, he nodded. "One week," he said. "But not until tomorrow. I need another day to prepare for this."

The doctor agreed. "Her potassium level is still a little high today. I ordered some medication to bring it down. I'll need to check her labs in the morning. If everything's within normal limits she'll be ready to go."

Jack nodded. "I'm not abandoning her," he said. "We just need a little time, a little rest, from this sickness."

In his head, he knew he had made the right decision for all of them, but in his heart, he knew only great loss and guilt.

"Dear God," he whispered, "please don't let her blame me."

Chapter Three

The Alzheimer's had crept in on Jack and Sara without any warning.

In the beginning, she forgot simple things and made mistakes anyone could make: losing track of her car keys, fumbling for words, forgetting important dates and deadlines. They blamed it on senioritis; after all, she was past sixty-five, a bona fide senior citizen. There was no family history of senility, so no cause for concern. An occasional mishap or slipup was no big deal. However, when her mistakes started to disrupt their daily routine, Jack's worries took off.

Some days she forgot to deposit their checks before sending out payment for the gas, electric, and charge cards. Creditors soon called to inform Jack their checks had bounced, and letters arrived from the bank citing "insufficient funds." Jack was mortified. He'd never bounced a check in his life.

"What happened here?" He dropped a letter in Sara's lap

She examined the paperwork, bewilderment etched across her face. "It must be a mistake," she said. "I made a deposit just last week." She searched through her bookkeeping, riffling through the stack of bills and their checkbook. "Oops," she said when she found the cash and checks in the bottom of her pocketbook, buried under keys, candy, brochures, and scraps of paper. "Guess I never made it to the bank. Sorry."

Jack took over the checkbook.

She came home from grocery shopping without half of the items on her list and bags stuffed with products they'd never use.

"Why did you buy Trix cereal?" Jack asked.

Sara picked up the box of cereal, mystified. "Somebody must have stuck it in my shopping cart by mistake," she answered.

Useless products began crowding their kitchen cupboards, and Jack started supervising her trips to the supermarket.

She left lists scattered around the house, scraps of paper with instructions for simple things. Jack found them in her pockets, stuffed in drawers, on the floor. "Rose's house," read one, and gave explicit directions to Sea Song, the home of their dearest friends, Rose and

Stan Fantagucci. She'd written "Laundry" on another in a shaky script, with step-by-step instructions on how to do a load of laundry. She'd scribbled "phone numbers" on another. At the top of the list was the number to Blue Hydrangeas. Puzzled, he scratched his head.

"What are these?" He laid the notes on the table where Sara was busy organizing a stack of photographs into an album.

She glanced at the slips of paper then pushed them away. "Oh, that," she said. "It's rubbish. You can throw it out."

"But why did you write these things down?"

"They're just notes. Forget about it," she replied, annoyance creeping into her voice.

"I don't get it. It's not like you don't know these things," he continued, determined to uncover her reasons for writing the notes.

She ignored him and continued with her project.

"Sara? Answer me," he said.

She threw the photos onto the table. "Leave me alone," she cried. "They're some things I wrote down, in case I forget."

"Forget our phone number? Forget how to wash a load of clothes?"

"Can't you drop it?" she asked. "I told you what they are. Now leave me alone. I want to finish this." She glared at him and he backed down, filing the notes in a desk drawer and never mentioning them again.

Some days, after his golf game, he sauntered in around noon expecting lunch and found her where he'd left her hours ago, sitting at the kitchen table, the newspaper scattered all over, her coffee cold and covered with a white film. The breakfast dishes still lay on the table with pieces of scrambled eggs stuck fast to the plates and silverware. The coffeemaker simmered on the countertop, the smell of burnt coffee in the air.

"What's going on?" The messy kitchen caught him by surprise.

"Back so soon, Jack?" She looked like she'd just woken up, eyes puffy, hair loose about her face, frizzy and tangled.

He pointed at the kitchen clock. "It's after noon, Sara. What have you been doing all morning?"

She stared back at him with bottomless eyes, their jewel-like intensity empty and dull. She picked up sections of the newspaper and arranged them in a neat pile. "I guess I've been waiting for you," she said.

"Since when do you wait for me? What about the dishes? What about lunch? What about our guests?" He fired questions at her, his tone tight with anxiety.

"The guests?" Her face was blank. "Well, I suppose they've gone out." She spoke with a tremor that revealed her uncertainty. Before he could ask any more questions, her eyes brightened. The tense lines around her mouth softened. "That's right," she said, her voice growing confident. "They asked about pottery. I directed them to Chatham." She handed him the newspaper. "Here, you read it. I can't seem to concentrate this morning."

"No thanks," he said. "I read it. What's for lunch?"

"Is it lunchtime? I forgot all about it." She left the table and rummaged through the refrigerator. "There's some leftover salad and grilled chicken. Is that okay?"

"Fine," he answered, relieved she'd returned to herself. "You had me going there for a minute. I thought you'd lost it," he said.

"Blame it on senioritis," she joked, and they laughed.

Months passed, and Sara's forgetting and odd behavior became more frequent. They continued to laugh at her senioritis, but soon it wasn't funny anymore.

Weeds choked the gardens, plants failed to thrive, and their beautiful hydrangeas turned pale and lifeless. The inn started to look shabby. Jack quit his golf league and stayed home to oversee the house and yard work, once Sara's duty. He ignored her objections and hired a professional grounds crew. She fumed while they resuscitated her landscape, but was delighted to see it all spring back to life.

"I can't get anything done around here," she complained as he followed her around while she went about her chores. "You're in my way."

"That's not how you do that." She criticized the way he folded laundry, vacuumed the rugs, or mopped floors. "Let me do it. Why are you always underfoot? Don't you have something else to do?"

He avoided arguments at all costs and allowed her to complete the task. When she left the room, he remade the bed, reorganized the kitchen, or washed the floor again.

Several months of shouldering this burden convinced him that keeping a twelve-room house had become too much for them, even with their part-time seasonal help. Sara flitted from one task to another, leaving things half-done or undoing his work. The house was unpresentable, and they had a reputation to maintain. Chagrined to admit it, he blamed it on their advanced age and hired the woman who helped them in the summer season to work year-round. Amelia Wright was a local woman from Mashpee, recommended by a friend at the golf club. She took over most of the housework and some of the cooking, and Jack and Sara welcomed the respite.

However, as the Alzheimer's dug its roots deeper into the recesses of Sara's mind, Jack's problems multiplied.

Leaving her home alone made him uncomfortable. He never knew what he'd find when he walked back in the door. She might be in a dead sleep, and struggle to climb out of it, dragging herself around for the rest of the day, lifeless.

She might be in a frenzy of activity, tearing a room apart, hunting for some object they hadn't seen in years, and abandoning the mess when she forgot what she was searching for. He spent hours picking up after her.

She might not be home at all, which terrified him. If her car was also missing, he called all around town, trying to track her down. If she was on foot, he drove through their development in search of her. Each time, she returned safe, surprised at his distress.

"Don't wander off without telling me where you're going," he admonished her.

"Come on, Jack, I'm not a child," she answered, annoyed. "You act like I don't know what I'm doing."

"I mean it, Sara. Leave a note. I worry when I come home and can't find you."

"You're getting a little nutty, Jack."

He hired a woman named Margie to stay with her while he went out. Margie was patient and kind. A homemaker all her life, she was a recent widow, her children scattered all across New England. She needed to earn a few dollars to stay afloat and worked as a companion for several elderly people. She was reliable, and Jack knew he left his wife in capable hands.

"Why is she here? Do you think I need a babysitter?" Sara asked, insulted.

"I thought you might like some company while I'm out. She can help with the business, answer the phone, take reservations. Give her a chance. She's nice."

"I can certainly manage without you for an hour or two," she said. "I don't need her around."

"Please, Sara. Do it for me," he begged, desperate to avoid another argument.

"It's a waste of money," she huffed.

But, to her surprise, Sara found she liked Margie and soon forgot her annoyance. Margie helped her manage the inn's business and kept her occupied while Jack played golf, shopped, or ran errands. The two of them walked through Sara's gardens, and Margie listened as she correctly named each flower and bush and described how she'd acquired and nurtured it. Her memory remained remarkable for such things, and most of the time she was right, but Margie, a fellow Master Gardener, recognized when Sara mixed up her facts. Careful not to provoke her, she subtly corrected her and allowed her to continue with her lecture for as long as she liked.

On sunny days, they sat in the garden while Margie read aloud the poems and short stories Sara enjoyed. They perused Sara's treasured photo albums for hours, discussing her family and their trips and adventures. Before they knew it, Jack was back.

Yet in spite of all of Jack's solutions to his most immediate problems, things grew more distressing when Sara failed to attend to her own personal needs.

She ate less than a bird if he didn't sit with her and watch every bite. She rejected many foods once eaten with gusto. She lost a few pounds, and didn't have many to spare. Jack catered to her whims, prepared six small meals a day, serving pudding and yogurt, cold cereal, soft fruits, and cooked vegetables. He supplemented milkshakes with protein powder. He made sure she took her vitamins. Before long, she returned to a stable weight and her complexion was clear and rosy.

She developed an aversion to water and wouldn't bathe for days. Jack was shocked. She'd always kept herself so nice.

"Did you take a shower?" he asked after she emerged from their bathroom with her hair dry and uncombed. He noted a faint odor of urine.

"Of course," she said.

"You don't look like you showered," he said. She wore yesterday's dirty clothes and he noticed holes in her socks. He shook his head, wondering where she found these old pieces of clothing. "The bathroom doesn't look like you showered, either. It's dry as a bone in there." He sighed. "Let's go." He escorted her into the shower where he soaped her from head to toe and then toweled her dry. They hadn't showered together in years, but he made a game of it and she laughed it off.

A private person, Jack kept his fears and concerns for Sara to himself. The key people in their lives were unaware of his troubles. It was easy to keep his secret. David was busy in Boston, raising a family and building a career. Sara's sister, Emily, was in New York with her family. He had no family. His brothers and sisters had passed away, and their survivors had spread all over the country. Socializing with friends had dwindled down to rare occasions. He frequented the golf club when he could, but hurried home as soon as it was politely possible.

For most of her life Sara had been a commercial artist, and throughout this early stage of Alzheimer's kept up with her painting. She often worked in her attic studio for hours, but the quality of her work began to suffer. She missed deadlines with the greeting card and publishing companies for whom she freelanced. Clients returned completed projects, claiming them not up to par. Sara pooh-poohed their concerns, said they were crazy, and vowed she'd never lift a paintbrush for any of them again. However, when the occasional call came for one of her exquisite florals, she forgot her frustration with the client and accepted the work.

One day, during his struggle to come to terms with her forgetfulness and confusion,

Jack sought her opinion on some issue and climbed up to her studio. She was in the throes of designing greeting cards for a major manufacturer. The offer came unexpectedly. She hadn't worked in months. Jack thought it would be good for her, but the deadline was nearing and she'd fallen behind schedule. The client called every other day for an update. He overheard their conversations and Sara sounded confident, assuring the client the project was going well.

Jack reached the door of the studio and peeked in, reluctant to interrupt her concentration. He'd always respected her workspace and gave her complete solitude when at work.

She stood poised in front of a canvas filled with a Nantucket Lightship Basket overflowing with blue hydrangeas. Her paintings of the vibrant summer flowers arranged with the hand-woven baskets that symbolized Nantucket Island had always been best sellers. Jack smiled as he approached her, entranced by the expression on her face, her absorption, and her pleasure in her work. Then he turned and saw the studio contained canvas after canvas of the same flowers, in the same basket, on the same-checkered tablecloth. The paintings were disappointing, poor work, but then he remembered it was Sara's work and let out an almost inaudible moan.

She heard him and welcomed him into the studio. "Hello, darling," she said, cheerfully. "I'm almost done. How do you like them?"

"Are these the paintings for the card company?" he stammered.

She nodded. "Yes, I wanted some with the lightship baskets and the flowers. They sell so well. I made a few of them, see?" She gestured toward the canvases strewn about the room.

Jack counted at least a dozen, all of them the same scene with minor variations. This would not do. Her client wasn't expecting this at all. Speechless, he pretended to study each painting. At last, he said, "Sara, honey, I don't understand what you're trying to accomplish here. These paintings are all the same. Some of them are not even finished."

She dropped her palette and brushes on the paint-spattered table. Frowning, she stood with her hands on her hips and examined the paintings.

"What do you mean?" she asked.

Jack dreaded these moments—they could turn into such ugly scenes—but he accepted her challenge and circled the room, appraising each canvas before he turned to face her. "Sara," he whispered sadly. "Honey, they're all paintings of the same basket, the same flowers. It's the same scene again and again. Don't you see it?"

She ran her fingers across the braid draped over her left shoulder. With the other hand,

54

she tapped a nervous rhythm on the table. She approached each canvas and regarded it with intensity. The realization that Jack was right sunk in. She struggled to maintain her composure, but overcome with humiliation she lashed out at him.

"What do you know?" she shouted.

He flinched at the harshness of her voice. Gone was the familiar tone of love she had spoken with only a few moments before.

"You don't know what you're talking about," she railed. "What do you know about art? About anything? You know nothing. You stupid asshole," she screamed and ran from the room.

Jack listened, stunned, as she clattered down the stairs. In all of their years she'd never screamed at him with such fury, had never called him such a name. Dumbfounded, he leaned against the wall. The situation was out of control. He allowed her a few moments before following her downstairs.

He found her in the kitchen fumbling with the coffeemaker. She tried to drop a filter into the basket but her hands trembled. Coffee grounds littered the counter top. Tears streamed down her cheeks.

"Let me," he said. She avoided his touch as he sidled up beside her and removed the basket from her hands. He dropped the filter in and measured the coffee. Once it started dripping, he led her into the living room.

He sat beside her on the couch and wrapped her in his arms, still silent. Nothing he could do or say would right the situation. He held her tight. She remained rigid, but after a few minutes relaxed against him.

"I'm sorry," she whispered. "I don't know what happens to me. I get scared. I get all mixed up. You're right about the paintings. I don't know what I'm doing, and I don't know what to do about it."

He continued to hold her, running his hands up and down her back and across her shoulders in his tender way. "I know, honey," he said, trying to sound reassuring. "We'll find out what's wrong. I'm sure it's nothing serious. We'll find out and we'll fix it. You'll see. Everything will be all right."

Chapter Four

After meeting with Sara's case manager, Allison, once more, Jack left the hospital with a head full of questions and a handful of information touting the different care facilities in their area. He sat in his car for a few moments and perused the literature, but overwhelmed with his choices he put the glossy brochures and pamphlets on the passenger seat and headed home. On the way, his worries abounded— Where would Sara go? How would he find the right place? What would she say when he told her she wasn't coming home? That last question was the worst.

As he made his way back to Blue Hydrangeas, he passed Sea Song, a large Victorian gingerbread house with fourteen rooms and an acre of lush gardens. Like Jack and Sara, its owners had operated the house as a bed and breakfast for years. Rose and Stan Fantagucci were dear friends, peacefully coexisting with the Harmon's as competitive innkeepers until advanced age and health problems forced them to close their home to visitors. Rose and Stan had proven their friendship several times over, offering help and support when Jack needed it during this difficult time. He stopped the car and turned around, pulling into Sea Song's long driveway. He'd find answers to his questions here.

As he approached the house in its summer glory, he spotted his friends sitting on the front porch in wicker rockers. He waved to them and they gestured him over.

"How are you?" Rose called when he reached hearing distance. "How's Sara? I take it she's not home from the hospital yet."

"Not yet," he answered, climbing the four steps up to the porch. Mismatched rockers and colorful baskets of flowers gave it a whimsical appearance. Well-shaded, it overlooked a salt marsh teeming with terns, herons, kingfishers, and snowy egrets. He settled into an empty rocker.

"So, what's the word?" Rose asked.

Jack told them about Dr. Fallon's recommendation that he admit Sara to an assisted living facility.

"It's only for a week," he explained, "just a few days until she's back on her feet."

"Oh, Jack, I'm so sorry," Rose said, taking his hand. "Do you know which place?" There were at least a dozen on Cape Cod.

"I was hoping you could make a suggestion," Jack said, "maybe come with me and help make some inquiries." Rose had walked this path with her mother, who had also suffered from Alzheimer's.

"What about David?" she asked.

"He was here the other day. I haven't told him about this yet. I hate to bother him. He's so busy. I'll call him once everything's settled."

"Of course I'll help," Rose said. "When do we need to go?"

"Now," he said. "She has to go tomorrow."

"The old bum's rush," commented Stan. He was an overweight, balding man in the prime of his retirement years who'd had more than his share of medical problems. "These hospitals can't wait to get you in, and then they throw you out the moment they're finished with you."

"I guess she's well enough to leave the hospital but not strong enough to come home," Jack explained.

"Let me get my purse." Rose headed into the house.

Stan changed the subject, thrusting the newspaper at Jack. "Did you see this?" he asked. "The market's down again. I don't know how we'll survive if this keeps up." Stan, a retired investment banker, had spent his life analyzing the stock market and it provided him with a handsome income. He complained about its fluctuations daily.

The front door banged and Rose stepped on to the porch, purse in hand. "Oh, be quiet," she said, giving Stan a playful slap. "Who cares? It'll turn around tomorrow, or next week, or sometime." She turned to Jack, trying to hide an affectionate grin. "He's so negative," she whispered.

"I heard that," Stan said, ruffling his newspaper.

Jack laughed, used to their banter. He, too, followed the stock market, but didn't take it as seriously as Stan did. Unlike his old friend, he'd never been responsible for other people's money. His interest in financial affairs was purely selfish.

At the start of his career, Jack had prudently invested in his company's stock. American Pharmaceuticals was the first in the industry to develop breakthrough drugs for the treatment of heart disease in the 1960's and early 1970's. When they unleashed their blockbuster drugs on a needy market, his hard work and loyalty paid off, making him a wealthy man. He continued to watch the market, but he shared Rose's attitude.

"It'll come up tomorrow," he reassured Stan.

"It better," Stan said. "That assisted living place will cost you a fortune."

Jack's ears perked up. "What?"

"Oh, yeah, sometimes as much as fifty thousand bucks a year, right, Rose?"

"Hush, Stan." Rose swatted him with her purse. "Jack doesn't need to worry about that now. Sara's only going for a week." She exchanged a wary glance with her husband.

"Right," Stan said. "A week. You should be able to handle that. No worries, Jack."

"I don't know how I'm going to do this, Jack confided once he and Rose were in the car.

She patted his hand. "One step at a time," she said. "I know this is hard, Jack, but with Alzheimer's we're called to do hard things, make hard choices. It's not your fault. There's nothing anyone can do to stop this."

"But Sara—," he said tearfully, fumbling with the seat belt.

"Sara won't understand at first, but before you know it she'll adjust."

They stared at each other for a moment fraught with sadness.

"Enough talk," Rose said, settling into her seat. "Let's get going."

Once on the road, she directed him to Bayside Village Senior Living Center, a retirement community just fifteen minutes from Blue Hydrangeas that offered first-class condominiums, an assisted living center, and a 110-bed skilled nursing facility that specialized in Alzheimer's care. Rose's mother had spent her last years there.

"Nothing has changed," Rose said. "This place still looks new." Her mother had been an inaugural resident. "I wonder if I'll know any of the staff." She browsed through brochures promoting the facility's services while they waited in the hospitality suite for a tour.

Marlene McHale, the Admissions Director, had flaming red hair, an unhealthy tan, and too much enthusiasm. She smelled like cigarettes and suffered from a nagging cough. Rose kept pace with her, chattering all the way, as Marlene brought them on a tour of the property. Jack lagged behind, wondering how she was able to get around the place with her heavy legs and backside.

They examined the grounds, the gardens, and the residence itself. They found nothing objectionable. The place was clean, the staff friendly. The common areas were tastefully decorated and welcoming. A well-appointed dining room overlooked a carefully tended golf course. Still, Jack brooded. His mind wandered while the redhead made her sales pitch. He studied his fingernails and wondered what he was doing there. He glided through the interview zombie-like, disconnected from the conversation. He made no comments, offered no questions. He inspected the tiny private room with single bed, bureau, nightstand, and recliner, and struggled to maintain his composure.

Marlene showed them one of several small apartments designed for couples. Each had a galley kitchen, dining area, living room, bedroom, and bath. Cheerfully decorated, it came furnished, but the redhead explained that most couples preferred to bring in their own furnishings. Rose, charmed by the cozy apartment, asked several questions. Marlene mentioned it was available. Rose didn't ask why.

Jack tuned out, thinking of their comfortable home a few miles away. He didn't want to be here, none of this was his plan, yet it was happening and he was powerless to stop it. Bayside Village was the closest facility to their home and happened to be one of the finest in the state. He had to accept it. He let Rose do all the talking, and spoke for the first time at the end of the interview.

"Will she be allowed to paint?" he asked. "Sara's an artist, you know, quite famous in these parts. She can't live without her painting."

"Well, that's wonderful," Marlene said. "We have many artists staying with us. In fact, we offer classes on Monday mornings in our studio. Your wife will have plenty of opportunities to continue her work."

Jack nodded, pleased. At least he could give her this one small pleasure.

He and Rose left Bayside Village with a handful of brochures and an application for admission.

"That wasn't so bad," Rose said as they headed for Jack's car.

Jack grunted. "Easy for you to say."

Rose regarded him over the rim of her bifocals. "Excuse me?"

"I'm sorry, Rose," he stammered, mortified by his callous remark. "Please, forgive me. This day has been more than I can handle."

Rose stopped walking and took Jack by the hand. "Let's take a break." She led him to a small table and chairs set up under a towering maple tree and they sat down.

"This *is* different for you, I know," she said. "I did this for my mother—"

Jack interrupted. "I'm not trying to minimize what you went through."

"I know, Jack, but Sara's your wife. You had plans for these years, and look what happened. I'm lucky I had Stan to help with my mother. It was rough at the end. She was physically and verbally abusive, pinching and slapping me when I tried to help her with bathing and dressing. She cursed at me with awful words I'd never heard her use before. It was devastating. She'd always been such a kind, gentle woman.

"To make matters worse, she was diabetic and refused to allow me to monitor her blood sugar levels or her diet. I had no choice, Jack.

As much as I wanted her to stay with me, it was impossible. Thank God for the nurses at Bayside Village. From day one, I never had to worry again."

Jack had heard this story before, from Rose and from others he'd met at the Alzheimer's support group she'd introduced him to. Although other people's stories made him feel less alone, they did nothing to ease his anxiety or his pain.

"Sara's not going to like this."

"She'll adjust, Jack, trust me."

"It's very quiet here," Jack noted. "Where is everyone?"

"It's after lunch," Rose answered. "Many of the residents go to their rooms for a nap or they're attending activities inside."

"There's a lot of ground for walking. She'll like that."

"She'll need an attendant. She won't be allowed to wander out here on her own."

"I hope not," Jack said. "She gets lost in our own house. That's the biggest part of the problem. She's a wanderer. My worst fear is she'll walk off and I won't find her before something terrible happens." He sighed. "You think this is the right place?"

"That's your call. We can visit some of the others if you'd like."

"I'm tired," Jack said. The prospect of visiting more facilities disheartened him. "This is okay.

I'll go home and start the paperwork. After all, it's only for a week."

Chapter Five

When at last it came time to reveal his concerns about his wife, Jack didn't know where to turn. He had a few close friends he could confide in, but he didn't feel comfortable discussing such personal information with any of them, and he didn't want to alarm his son or Sara's sister with his worries in case it all turned out to be nothing. There could be a reasonable explanation for what was happening—simple old age, a vitamin deficiency, a thyroid imbalance—but deep in his heart, he knew speaking up about Sara's odd behavior would open a Pandora's Box.

With some trepidation, he called their physician and brought up his worries. Dr. Fallon asked a few probing questions and said he wanted to see Sara in his office. Jack made an appointment for the following Monday morning.

His discussion with Dr. Fallon unsettled him even more. He felt like a traitor, as though he'd dishonored his wife to suggest something was wrong with her mind. Sara was brilliant and accomplished, a respected artist, a successful businesswoman, a Master Gardener, and the perfect hostess. She was a healthy woman, never sick, taking no medications. The only time she'd ever spent in a hospital was when the children were born. She never missed her annual physical, took her vitamins and calcium tablets, and walked every day, rain or shine.

He was the one with the medical problems. A battalion of pills filled their medicine chest, powerful drugs to keep his heart healthy and strong. He had some prostate trouble, but nothing too serious; after all, he was almost seventy. Most men his age had prostate trouble. He took a pill for that, too. He watched what he ate, kept an eye on his weight, and made sure his ankles didn't swell too much. He put away the saltshaker and drank his brandy and California wine in moderation. Dr. Fallon proclaimed him as healthy as he could be, considering his age and medical history.

While they waited for the appointment with Dr. Fallon, Sara's condition improved, and they enjoyed a string of good days, when her mind seemed clearer and she did not become mixed up too often. They worked side-by-side preparing the gardens and readying the house for the pending cold weather. Jack grew optimistic: maybe whatever virus or imbalance she'd struggled with had run its course.

The night before the appointment with Dr. Fallon, they made a delicious dinner of roast chicken with mashed potatoes and gravy, and a tossed salad dressed with their homemade vinaigrette. They uncorked a delightful bottle of Chardonnay. After dinner, they ate chocolate ice cream for dessert. Sara brought out some of her old photo albums and they relived the years of renting their summerhouse on Corn Hill Beach in Truro. The photographs were of good times, happy times, of picnics at the beach and building sandcastles, and filled them with a deep sense of satisfaction.

They skipped the eleven o'clock news and climbed into bed, clinging to each other in the dark. He held her in his arms, content in the soothing rhythm of her breath, tickling him as it drifted across his shoulder. They were asleep before midnight.

Come daylight, everything had changed. Jack woke and found her gone. He leaped out of bed, threw on his clothes, and started searching the house, checking for her in the bathroom, the upstairs bedrooms, downstairs. He couldn't find her anywhere.

He climbed the two flights to her studio. As usual, the door was closed but unlocked. He knocked before opening it and stepped into the quiet, lifeless room, where the insistent tap of rain against glass summoned him to the window. From the attic studio, he looked down upon their grounds, shrouded in fog. It was early autumn, the trees showing just a hint of foliage. The nasty weather made him uneasy. He hurried out of the room and dashed downstairs.

A chilly draft greeted him as he entered the kitchen and saw the sliding door to the deck was unlatched. *Is Sara outdoors in this wretched rain?* he thought. *Has she gone for a walk? She never takes her walk until after her first cup of coffee.* He noted the automatic coffeepot, silent on the kitchen counter, too early to brew. He ignored the rising panic in his gut and dressed for the weather, grabbing his jacket and putting on shoes before heading out the back door.

Jack circled the house, shouting her name. He didn't find her in the cutting garden or in the back yard. He worked his way down the driveway, feeling foolish for panicking. She'd probably decided to take her walk before breakfast. Still, a troublesome thought in the back of his mind suggested this was not the case.

Sara had several routes to walk throughout the development. She used the established walking paths, but also traveled along the main streets, admiring her neighbor's homes and gardens and stopping to chat with anyone she passed.

Jack took off along this route. He walked quickly and saw no one. With each step he tried to convince himself he worried for nothing, praying at any moment he'd turn a corner and see her coming toward him, a smile on her face, eager to tell him about a bird she'd observed or a new planting in someone's yard. He didn't see her.

As he approached the path to Falmouthport Beach, he paused, ready to turn back because Sara avoided the beach, complaining it was too breezy, especially when it was raining. Walking on sand was a struggle and she feared losing her balance. She preferred to stay on the road where the ground was level.

However, at the last moment something urged him to head for the shore. He quickly made his way there, the wind pushing against him. The tide was rolling in and the sound of crashing waves drowned out everything else. The beach was deserted. He shielded his eyes with his hands and searched the coastline.

She stood at the edge of the surf, her thick, white hair loose and flowing in the wind, whipping about her face, her legs splayed, her arms held out for balance. The open ocean rolled and churned toward her, making her seem small and frail. He raced toward her, screaming her name. She turned at his voice and stumbled, falling into the water, landing on her hands and knees.

He plunged into the water and wrapped his arms around her, pulling her to her feet. "My God, Sara, what are you doing out here?" he asked, breathless from his efforts. He rubbed her arms in a desperate attempt to make her warm.

"I don't know," she cried. "I'm all mixed up."

The frigid water soaked through his shoes and socks. She shivered against him, her thin, flannel nightgown plastered against her body. He covered her with his jacket and led her away from the water. They labored across the beach to the path that led home.

He draped an arm over her shoulders and they stumbled back to the house. It seemed to take forever. Sara shivered uncontrollably, short of breath, her chest heaving. Jack struggled with every step, winded by the exertion of holding her up and propelling her forward. The rain continued to pelt them, but it had subsided a bit and they were able to maneuver through it with little difficulty.

They finally arrived home. He guided her through the front door and into the family room where he removed her wet nightgown, covered her with a blanket, and led her to the couch, easing her onto the soft cushions.

She cried, making little gasping sounds and repeating, "I'm so mixed up," in a pitiful voice that chilled him to his core.

He made coffee, brought her a cup, and held it to her lips. She sipped carefully and flopped back against the couch, her blue eyes shiny with tears.

"Oh, Jack," she moaned. "What's happening to me?"

Later that day, Jack watched while Dr. Fallon grimly examined Sara, took samples of her blood, and performed a few mental tests. When the examination was over, he brought them into his office and tried to be optimistic, but warned them the situation could be grave. Following his recommendations, they consulted a neurologist and a psychiatrist. She went for a MRI of her brain.

Several stressful weeks passed before all of the test results and consultation reports were in. They returned to Dr. Fallon's office and he explained the diagnosis. He was blunt, left no room for misunderstanding, and told them what to expect.

Jack refused to believe it. "I want a second opinion," he said. "I want her to see the best specialists we can get. We'll go to Boston, to New York. Nobody in our family has ever had Alzheimer's disease. Find something else. You have to do more tests."

Sara sat by his side and clung to his hand. An air of despondency descended upon her. Silent, she studied the doctor's face.

"I wish I could tell you otherwise, Jack, but there is no single test to diagnose Alzheimer's," Dr. Fallon explained. "We've done all the tests available to rule out other conditions that might explain Sara's symptoms. Everything indicates probable Alzheimer's, and there's nothing more to do."

"You say it's 'probable,'" Jack argued. "See? You're not sure. It could be something else."

Dr. Fallon leaned toward Jack and looked deep into his eyes. "Jack, right now all I can say is that it *is* probable, because only an autopsy can provide a definitive diagnosis."

Jack had no words to respond to that suggestion.

The doctor wrote a prescription for a medication that might slow the progression of the disease and they agreed to try it.

"Sara," Dr. Fallon said, turning toward her, "the best you can do is live one day at a time, and try to maintain as much of your routine and lifestyle as possible." He encouraged them to go on with the operation of their bed and breakfast for as long as they felt able, and he urged Sara to continue with her artwork.

The next day, Jack visited the library and asked the librarian to point him in the direction of the books on Alzheimer's disease. He spent hours holed up in a corner of the reference section poring through textbooks, medical journals, and self-help guides. As he studied the reading material, he realized how much he did not know about this illness. He read with uninterrupted concentration, and did not like what he learned.

Sara was but one of an estimated 5.1 million Americans with probable Alzheimer's.

There is no cure.

Damage to the brain may start a decade or more before problems become evident. Jack thought back over the last few years, trying to pinpoint the first time Sara showed any sign that this monster disease had settled inside that brilliant brain of hers. He shook his head. He had not seen this coming, not until it was well on its way. Perhaps if he had paid closer attention to her senioritis they may have been able to staunch its spread.

As Alzheimer's progresses, he learned, people may be unable to recognize family and friends. They may be unable to carry out tasks that involve multiple steps such as getting dressed, or cope with new situations. They may suffer from hallucinations, delusions, and paranoia, and behave impulsively.

In its late stages, the person becomes completely dependent on others for all aspects of their physical care, and may be bedridden most or all of the time as the body slowly and painfully shuts down.

Deep into his reading, he came upon a chilling fact: those with Alzheimer's may live, on average, just three to nine years from diagnosis. This information brought tears to his eyes, and he closed the book, staring at the desktop, willing the tears not to spill and his heart not to break.

Three to nine years, he thought. *That's all.*

Terrified by the horrible facts about Alzheimer's and the future it predicted, Jack set about disproving Dr. Fallon's diagnosis. He wouldn't give up.

He and Sara consulted the top specialists in Boston and New York and heard the same thing: Sara most likely had Alzheimer's, and little could be done. They advised him to prepare for the changes that would occur, to provide his wife with a safe environment and a plan to ensure her comfort and dignity in her final days. The idea of making such arrangements galled him. He didn't know how or where to begin. He stalled, certain there was plenty of time for all of that.

Life went on, and Sara improved on the medication. Jack breathed a sigh of relief, convinced they could conquer this illness with pharmaceuticals. He took control of everything, watching over her and managing their bed and breakfast business, the housekeeping, the bills, all the minute details of their lives.

Yet, as determined as Jack was to continue with life as usual, the Alzheimer's made the daily operation of the bed and breakfast more and more impossible.

Sara began to make errors, and soon he couldn't trust her to follow through on phone calls, reservations, and special requests. She forgot to collect payments from guests and sometimes misplaced them when she did. Jack started to find checks in the wastebasket and resigned himself to sift through the trash every day for cash, checks, or credit card payments she might have thrown away. During their last season, she made a disastrous error that convinced him their inn-keeping days would soon end.

Late June and the roses were blooming. The air was warm with the promise of summer days. It was a busy month at the inn. Blue Hydrangeas catered to an adult clientele free to take off at a whim for a getaway week or weekend. In early summer, golfers, antique hunters, artists, and honeymooners occupied all four of its rooms.

Jack was at home alone one Saturday afternoon waiting for Sara to come back from shopping with Rose when a knock at the front door interrupted his reading. He didn't expect anyone. The house had been booked for weeks and all guests had checked in.

A young couple stood on the porch, their backs to the door as they admired Sara's hydrangeas. They stood close together, wrapped up in each other, and Jack guessed they were newlyweds. He smiled before he spoke, enjoying the privilege of witnessing their happiness.

"May I help you?" He opened the door. Three suitcases and a garment bag rested on the porch.

The couple turned to him with unabashed joy. "We're the Rowley's, Kevin and Kim," the young man explained, "and we have a reservation."

"Newlyweds, huh?"

They nodded, glanced at each other, and smiled shyly. Kim linked her arm through Kevin's and held on tight.

"We were married last night," the bride answered, a hint of a blush suffusing her cheeks.

They couldn't have been more than twenty-two, twenty-three, Jack surmised, probably straight out of college. "A reservation?" he asked. "For this weekend?"

"No, sir," Kevin answered. "For the whole week. It's our honeymoon. Kim's grandfather gave it to us for a wedding gift. He said you know him, Ben Davenport, from Monroe, New York. He said he used to work with you."

The name sounded familiar. Jack thought back to the company and recalled a man named Davenport in Research and Development, a heavy hitter, maybe a vice president.

As the memory of Ben Davenport flooded his consciousness, he grabbed hold of the door and steadied himself. Davenport had been more than a coworker. They'd attended conferences and conventions together, played in the company's golf league, and shared the ride back and forth to the New Jersey head office for years. They'd socialized with their wives, taking them out for dinner and dancing. Sara had been fond of Ben and his wife, Marian. Ben Davenport was a friend, one he hadn't seen or heard from in almost twenty years.

"Certainly I remember Ben," he said. "How is he?"

"He's great," Kim replied. "Still in the same house, still playing cards and golf. He said to say hello to you."

"And Marian?"

Kim turned away, her expression quickly changing from joy to grief.

"Marian passed away recently," Kevin answered. "Cancer."

"I'm sorry," Jack replied, feeling sympathy for his old friend, and remembering Marian as a sweet woman with a lovely disposition.

"Anyway," Kevin went on, "Ben reserved a week's stay here for our wedding gift. He said we'd have a great time and you'd treat us right. So, here we are, and we've had a long drive."

"Come on in." Jack opened the door. "I'll fix you a cold drink and we'll get you checked in."

They followed him through the house to a screened-in porch in the back. A towering oak shaded the room and there was a light breeze. He left them to get comfortable and went to the kitchen where he poured two glasses of iced tea and arranged a plate of Sara's homemade oatmeal cookies. After serving his guests, he went to the office and pulled out the guest registry. He scanned the list of reservations for that day, that week, and confirmed his fears were well founded: the Rowley's had no reservation, and the house had no vacancy.

He turned to the pile of checks stored in the top desk drawer, deposits on reservations. He found Ben Davenport's check close to the bottom. In the corner, Ben had written the dates he'd reserved: June 22 to 29. The kids were right. Sara had made an error, a big mistake. Ben had made and paid for a week's reservation. He must have called and she had never told Jack. She must have forgotten to write it into the book and given the room to someone else. He noted the date on the check: February 15.

"Oh, Sara, love, you've done it this time," he said. Sara had messed up reservations before. She made arrangements with people and failed to record them. She forgot phone calls and misplaced checks. People showed up at their door expecting a room. Jack had no idea they were coming, but somehow a room had always been available and things had worked out. Now, he had nothing.

How could he fix this? He couldn't turn this young couple away, not Ben's granddaughter, not on their honeymoon. The kids were exhausted. He knew how draining the trip from

New York to Falmouthport could be, especially on a Saturday; he'd done it too many times himself.

He examined his options. He could call Sea Song to ask if the Fantagucci's had anything open. Then he remembered Rose mentioning they also had a full house this week.

The innkeeper's association might know of a vacancy, but he rejected that idea as well. If he directed the Rowley's somewhere else, he'd have to explain the mix-up. The kids would be disappointed and Ben would be upset. Jack would never offend an old friend.

In addition to their four guest rooms were the rooms reserved for David, Anne, and the boys. They were functional, but nothing special, and certainly not suitable for guests. Sara had poured her heart and soul into the guest rooms, made them warm and welcoming, what one expected at a Cape Cod bed and breakfast. Only one other room in the house had the same charm as the guest rooms, and that was their room.

It could work. Mrs. Wright had been in just a few hours earlier and given the room a thorough cleaning. The linens were fresh. The bathroom was spotless. He'd pile all of their personal belongings in the boys' rooms and they'd stay in David and Anne's room. The Rowley's could have the master bedroom for the week. It was the best room in the house.

Sara wouldn't like it, he suspected, but it was her own fault. He'd try to make an adventure out of it.

He joined the honeymooners on the porch. "I have to apologize. I know you've had a long drive and you're ready to relax and get started on your vacation, but I had a problem with the help and I'm a little behind schedule. The room isn't ready. I'll have it put together in about a half an hour. In the meantime, why don't you take a walk on the beach?"

Refreshed from their cookies and tea, the young couple agreed and asked for directions. Jack sent them on their way and dashed upstairs to get to work.

What was once a pleasure and a joy had become a chore and a burden. Jack couldn't run Blue Hydrangeas, accommodate guests, and take care of Sara. He would have to close the inn. It would break Sara's heart. He didn't know what they would do in the big old house all alone. It was happening slowly, but he could see all that they'd worked for slipping through his   hands.

Chapter Six

Sara reached over to pat the other side of the bed, her fingers searching for the reassuring form usually lying beside her. Her hand dropped to the mattress with a thud; no one there.

Puzzled, she sat up and called, "Hello," but there was no reply, no sound, except for the drone of the air conditioner.

Moonlight filtered through a narrow opening in the drapes, filling the room with a soft glow, revealing unfamiliar objects: a chair, a small table, a television hanging from the wall. Something was wrong. She stroked the sheets covering the small bed. Cool and coarse, they reeked of bleach. This wasn't her bed. This wasn't her bedroom.

"Where am I?" she wondered aloud.

Raising her arms high over her head, she gave a great yawn and stretched. A bright light outside the open door caught her attention. *There,* she thought, *he's out there.* Lowering her legs over the side of the bed, she felt for her slippers with her toes and stepped into them. Standing with great care, she began to walk toward the door. An earsplitting noise pierced the silent room.

She cried out, wrapping her hands around her ears to stifle the painful racket.

A large woman in white pushed open the door, summoned by the alarm that alerted the nursing staff a patient at risk for falls had left her bed. She switched on the light, and then turned off the alarm.

Sara blinked in the brightness and shielded her eyes with her hands.

"Where are you going, Sara? It's the middle of the night. Are you looking for the bathroom?" The woman's voice was as soft and gentle as powder.

Sara peered through her fingers until her vision adjusted to the light, and then lowered her hands to her sides.

The strange woman took her by the arm and led her toward the bathroom.

Sara shook her head. "No." She wrenched her arm away and raised her fist, blocking the woman from grasping her arm again. "Let me go. I have to find him."

"Find who?" asked the woman.

Sara paused for a moment, her thoughts churning like a whirlpool. "You know," she stammered. "That man. The one who was here before."

"Your husband?" asked the woman. "Jack?"

Sara's eyes lit up with understanding. "Yes, Jack."

"Jack's not here, Sara. He's at home and sound asleep, I hope."

"Of course he's not sleeping," Sara said, affronted. "We have to make breakfast."

The woman sighed and shook her head. "Sara," she explained with great patience. "It's four o'clock in the morning. Everyone's asleep, and you should be, too. Let me help you back into bed." She reached for the old woman's arm.

Sara pulled away. "Wait a minute," she ordered. "Don't you know we have work to do? If we don't get started, nothing will be prepared for our guests when they wake up."

The woman stared at her, hands on her hips. She wore an ID badge that read *Rita Malone, RN*.

Sara didn't know this woman. She didn't know any *Rita Malone, RN*. "Who are you?" she asked. "What are you doing in my house?" She took stock of the unfamiliar room. Nothing was right. This wasn't her house. "Where am I?" she shouted, clutching her nightgown. Her voice warbled, betraying her fear. "What is this place?"

The woman spoke to her kindly. "Sara, you're in the hospital, and I'm Rita, the night nurse. You're all right, Sara. You're safe here." She smoothed down the front of her immaculate uniform. "I'll tell you what," she said. "Come sit with me at the nurses' desk. I'll make you a nice hot cup of my special chamomile tea, and we'll see if you won't get back to sleep." She reached for Sara's hand.

Lulled by Rita's mellow tone, Sara allowed her to walk her to the nurses' desk. Rita settled her into a cushiony vinyl recliner, wrapped a blanket around her, and positioned a small table across her lap.

"Sit right here and I'll get you that cup of tea," she said.

Sara appraised her surroundings while she waited. *The hospital,* she thought, *that's where I am.* She couldn't remember how she'd gotten there. *I must be sick,* she surmised, and ran her fingers through her hair. The evening before, someone, not that man, not Jack, had pulled out her French braid and brushed her long white hair. Whoever it was had done a lousy job. It was tangled and unruly.

While waiting for Rita, she fidgeted with her hair, her nightgown, and the blanket. She fidgeted a lot these days, even she saw that, but she was so nervous all of the time, and lost track of so many things. Crowds of people terrified her. Loud noises overwhelmed her. Simple tasks were impossible. She struggled to

86

keep up, but people rushed her, raced around her, left her behind, and left her out. Why? She didn't know.

A young woman pulled up a chair beside her and sat down with a groan. She was heavyset and dressed in a hot pink nurse's uniform. She wore her name embroidered on her blouse: "Maria Cortez, Nursing Assistant."

"I'm beat," she said, yawning. She turned toward Sara. "I see you're up again tonight, Mrs. Harmon." A Latin accent spiced her English, and Sara strained to follow her words. "Perhaps you'll sleep better when you go home and get in your own bed."

"That'll be soon," said Rita. She set the cup of tea and a handful of graham crackers on the tray table. Sara wrapped her hands around the steaming cup, soaking in its warmth. "She's for discharge in the morning."

"Hear that, Mrs. Harmon?" asked Maria. "You go home tomorrow. What will you do when you get home, first thing?"

"Oh, I don't know," replied Sara, wondering, *how will I get home? Where is home?* She abandoned the teacup, picked up a napkin and began shredding it. Her eyes darted from one nurse to the other.

Rita rescued her from her confusion. "Sara lives in Falmouthport, Maria, in a lovely home called Blue Hydrangeas. It's near the beach and has a beautiful garden. Her husband, Jack, will pick her up in the morning." She addressed Sara. "I bet he'll be glad to see you."

Sara's face was blank. "Jack?"

"Yes, Jack. Your husband. Remember him?"

Sara brightened, beaming. A wondrous smile lit up her face. *Of course! Jack. He'll bring me home.* "Oh, I haven't seen him in a long time," she told the nurses. "Does he know I'm here?"

"Of course he does," answered Rita. "He visits you twice every day and calls every night to say good night."

"He's my best friend," Sara said. Her eyes softened. A small smile tugged at her lips.

"And such a nice man," added Maria. "How long have you two been married?"

Sara thought for a moment, struggling to remember. "Oh, it's been a long time," she finally answered, "since after the war, World War Two. We got married in the spring. I wore my mother's wedding dress." She smiled at the memory.

After the nurses resumed their duties, Sara sipped her tea and nibbled on crackers.

Rita handed her a few sheets of paper and some pencils and she went to work. She sketched Rita talking on the phone. Her unsteady hand flowed over the paper, leaving behind shaky lines; a child's drawing, but a recognizable likeness. A vase of wilted flowers sat on the nurses' desk and she drew that, but in her drawing, the flowers seemed vibrant and alive, as though delivered just that afternoon.

At six o'clock, the hospital sprang to life. Maria walked her to her room, took her into the bathroom, and helped her bathe and use the toilet. She took Sara's clothes out of the closet and coached her while she put them on. She assisted her into the easy chair by the window, turned on the television, and placed the overbed table across her legs, making sure the call bell was within easy reach in case Sara needed a nurse.

At the clatter of the breakfast carts rolling down the hall and the chatter of the day shift coming on board, Maria said goodbye to Sara, wished her well, and moved on to other patients and duties.

A little later, Verlaine, the day shift nursing assistant, stopped in Sara's room with her breakfast tray.

"How are you this morning, Mrs. Harmon? Feeling better?" she asked as she opened the milk and juice containers.

"Oh, yes." Sara watched Verlaine butter her toast and fix her coffee. In the hospital, the girls fixed her meals because all of the little boxes and packages got her all mixed up.

"It's a beautiful day," Verlaine said, finished with her task. "You must be glad you're going home." She straightened the bedclothes.

"Jack is coming for me." Sara's eyes twinkled.

"Lucky you," Verlaine teased. "He's hot stuff."

"Hot stuff," Sara said, and laughed. The thought of Jack, an old man, as "hot stuff" amused her.

Verlaine left her alone and Sara ate her breakfast, one item at a time. Her sickness hadn't affected her appetite. She loved to eat, but her speedy metabolism prevented her from putting on weight, unlike Jack, who watched every bite, exercised like a fool, and packed on extra pounds anyway.

Finished with breakfast, she leaned back in the chair to watch TV, a morning talk show. She fidgeted with her snowy hair, twirling it absentmindedly around her finger, and fussed with her clothing, fastening and unfastening the buttons on her blouse.

The TV program grew monotonous, and her bottom was getting sore from sitting in such an uncomfortable chair. She picked up a magazine and leafed through its glossy pages. Bored, she threw it to the floor.

"Hello?" She directed her voice toward the door. "Are you there?" she called. No response, but she could hear the bustle of activity outside her room. People rushed through the corridor, alarms and telephones rang incessantly, and announcements blared from overhead speakers: "Dr. Tomlinson, line six." "X-ray STAT, room 443." All of this commotion made her nervous. She was a cluster of knots, a tangle of taut nerves, lost in her own surroundings.

The calendar on the wall caught her attention and she noted the date: Wednesday, July 10, summer. When she got home, she'd check the register to see who was staying with them. She'd bake some oatmeal cookies and brew sun tea out on the deck. The day would surely be a busy one.

As she considered her plans, it dawned on her that there were no guests and she had no work. Her beautiful bed and breakfast was no more. Jack had decided it was too much work for them and stopped inviting people to stay. This thought filled her with sadness. Opening her home to friends and guests had been an important part of her life, providing much pleasure and happy memories. She missed the activity, the company, the conversations, and the anticipation that accompanied each season.

She sat in the chair fidgeting and mumbling to herself, waiting for someone, anyone, to come. Jack took great care to see she had company all of the time and never left her unattended. Her isolation overwhelmed her and she called out again in a frantic voice.

"Nurse! Nurse!"

Footsteps hurried to her room and Verlaine popped in.

"Yes, Mrs. Harmon? What is it?"

"Where's Jack?" Sara clung to the young woman's hand.

"He'll be here any minute," Verlaine said. "Just a little while longer and he'll be here to take you home."

"I want to go home," Sara said, hanging her head, near tears. "I want to go home with Jack."

"Soon, Mrs. Harmon, soon," Verlaine assured her, stroking her snowy hair.

Chapter Seven

The heady aroma of fresh brewed coffee roused Jack from a restless sleep. He rolled over and checked the clock: 7:10.

"Sara?" He reached across the queen-size bed for her warm and familiar form. He'd awakened each day for the last fifty-four years with his wife snuggled tight against him, the cadence of her easy breathing reassuring him that the long night had passed and she lay safely beside him. He'd never tell anyone but it scared him to wake up alone, to find her half of the bed untouched and cold. His hand hit the mattress with a soft thump and he stifled a groan. Sara was gone, at least for another week, and, if their situation didn't improve, maybe for good.

He clutched her pillow, breathing in the soothing scent of her lavender shampoo. It calmed him for a moment, but then he threw

Marianne Sciucco

the pillow onto the floor and sat up. Waking up without Sara was something he had to get used to, even if he didn't want to.

Ignoring his stiff joints and the ache of his over-stretched bladder, he maneuvered himself out of bed and headed for the bathroom. He had no time to think or grieve. This was an important day. In a few hours, Sara would leave the hospital and he'd admit her to Bayside Village Senior Living Center.

He performed some stretching exercises, showered, and dressed in khaki shorts and a polo shirt. A tall man with broad shoulders, long legs, and a slight paunch, he had a commanding presence, although his age had caught up with him.

His hairline had started receding in his early fifties, and he was gray by sixty, but what hair remained was full and thick. Blue eyes peered out from behind a pair of stylish glasses. State of the art hearing aids hid in each ear, making it impossible to tell he had any impairment at all. He presented himself as well in control and self-possessed.

He couldn't believe a lifetime had passed. Blind to the signs of aging mapped over his face, he thought of himself as ageless, immortal. Whenever he caught a random reflection of his face, he stopped short and stared. *I'm almost eighty,* he marveled, *an octogenarian.* He'd outlived all of his brothers and sisters, and, in spite of the health

94

problems that had plagued him for years, felt indestructible.

Jack headed downstairs to the kitchen, grateful for the automatic coffee maker. The scent of freshly brewed Italian Roast grew stronger with each step.

At the bottom of the stairs, Sara's two cats howled their displeasure at having to wait for breakfast. He stepped around them, muttering, "Good morning to you, too," and set about serving them their kibble.

That chore completed, he opened the front door and picked up the newspaper. Back in the kitchen, he poured his first cup of coffee and took a sip before settling down at the breakfast table.

The eat-in kitchen was as his housekeeper, Amelia Wright, had left it the day before. The hardwood floors gleamed, the glass cabinets sparkled, and not a dish was out of place. It was a kitchen designed for the feeding of large groups of people. He and Sara had prepared delicious homemade breakfasts from that kitchen for many years: cranberry-orange pancakes, Eggs Benedict, omelets stuffed with fresh vegetables and gourmet cheeses, home-baked breads and muffins.

This morning's menu would be cold cereal and fresh fruit for one.

As he perused the morning news, footsteps rumbled down the back staircase. His grandson, Derek, entered the kitchen mumbling good morning. He was visiting for the summer and worked as a caddy and lifeguard at Jack's golf club. In his off time, he helped Jack with chores and kept an eye on his grandmother.

Derek parked in front of the refrigerator, door wide open, and yawned.

"Late night?" Jack asked.

Derek poured a large glass of orange juice and drank half in one gulp. "Yeah, a bunch of us caught a movie and played some pool afterward. I got in about midnight or so." He leaned against the kitchen counter, his mussed hair hiding his eyes. He brushed it away and squinted at the sunlight streaming through the window over the kitchen sink.

"Sounds like fun," Jack said, relieved that Derek and his friends led a benign social life and avoided drugs and booze. Kids got into so much trouble these days, as Derek's older brother, Jesse, had earlier that year. "Why are you up so early?"

"I booked a caddy job for eight o'clock."

"Excellent," Jack said. Derek was a hard worker.

"What's up with Grandma?" Derek asked. "Is she coming home today?"

"She's fine. She's leaving the hospital this morning, but she's not coming right home. She's going to one of those rest homes for a few days."

"Why?" Derek asked. "Is something wrong?"

"No, Dr. Fallon just thought a few more days rest and rehab and she'll be ready to come home. It's only for a week." Jack got up to pour his second cup of coffee.

"She never had to do that before," said Derek. "Has something changed?"

"Well, Derek," Jack said, sitting back at the table, "it changes every day, you see, her condition tends to fluctuate. It's all part of the disease. Right now, she's a little weak. That last fall really took the wind out of her sails. But, with some physical therapy, she'll get stronger. She'll get better and come home and everything will be all right."

"How are you feeling, Grandpa?" Derek asked. "Are you okay?"

"I guess so," Jack answered, unsure. He had many feelings about this day and couldn't begin to sort them out.

"How about I go with you? I can get someone to cover for me at work. We can bring Grandma to the place together. I'll drive."

The boy's earnestness touched Jack. Derek had just graduated high school and planned to start college in the fall. Jack studied him, admiring his lean physique rippled with the muscles of a swimmer. He resembled his father at that age, and reminded Jack his own son had once stood in the same way, against the same counter, and exhibited the same care and concern for others.

Jack shook his head. "I appreciate your help, but you need to go to work. Your father's on his way." He watched the boy toast a bagel and refill his glass.

"Call if you need me," Derek said over his shoulder as he left the kitchen. "You have my cell number."

"I promise," Jack replied.

He opened the sliding glass door and stepped onto the deck, releasing the two cats now fed and happy and clamoring to go out. Sara had found them shivering under a bush one misty, miserable morning years ago. Cleo, a lovely calico, was skittish, but warmed up once she grew comfortable with strangers. Buster, a golden tabby, was a real tomcat and boss of the house. Sara lived for those cats and they adored her, snuggling up with her whenever she sat down and sleeping on a pile of pillows next to her side of the bed. Jack held the door open and they scampered outside.

He followed them and planted himself in a deck chair, basking in the sun's warmth. He tasted salt in the air and licked his lips. When they'd bought the house in the early 1980's, ocean front property hadn't been important to them. The barely perceptible scent of the sea wafting in with the breeze was enough. Instead, Jack and Sara valued open space and privacy. Their home spread across two acres. The only sign of nearby neighbors was the pitch of an occasional rooftop visible through the white pines, red cedars, and oak trees bordering their property.

Jack nursed his coffee, the July sun warming his shoulders, and listened for the woodpeckers, wrens, and purple martins nestled in the maples and pines surrounding the house.

Even with the ominous task ahead, it promised to be a superb summer day.

When the phone rang he debated letting the answering machine pick it up, but a glance at the caller ID convinced him to answer on the third ring.

"Hello, Emily," he said to Sara's younger sister. Emily lived in upstate New York with her husband, Ed, and their large extended family of seven children and twenty-two grandchildren.

They'd last visited at Easter. It had been a stressful weekend. Emily had grilled Jack about Sara's condition, troubled by the dramatic changes she saw in her sister, who was more confused than usual and needed constant reassurance and direction. Jack dismissed her concerns, explaining Sara had been ill with an infection and was taking several new medications, and changed the subject. A worried Emily returned to New York and phoned Jack every other day to keep tabs on her sister.

"Is she home yet?" she asked.

"Not yet," Jack replied, and then told her his plans.

Emily was silent for a long moment, then asked, "Is that really necessary, Jack?"

"For a little while, just until she's back on her feet," he reassured her.

"Oh, I don't know. This seems pretty final to me."

"I haven't agreed to anything more than a week, Em," Jack said.

"Well, I guess you don't have too many options," she conceded. "You do what you have to do, Jack. Ed and I are here, any time you need us." She paused, and then asked, "What about you, Jack? How are you feeling?" They were fond of each other, like brother and sister.

Jack answered with his standard response to inquiries regarding him and his wife. "Everything's fine, Em. Everything's okay."

"How's Sara? Did you see her yesterday?"

"You bet. She's back on track, seems more like herself."

Emily breathed a sigh of relief. "What time are you picking her up?"

"I'm expected at the hospital by ten. We have an eleven o'clock appointment at the assisted living place."

"That ought to give you plenty of time," she said. "Please tell Sara I called. Tell her I'm praying for her. Tell her we love her. Eddie and I plan to visit in a few weeks. We'll let her get settled back at home, and we'll call to let you know when we're coming, okay?"

"Sure, Em, that'll be nice. I'll let Sara know you called. You have a good day, now. Give my best to Ed." Jack ended the call.

He finished his coffee and headed into the house. Seated at the kitchen table, he ate breakfast without tasting it and then washed the few dishes in the sink before setting out on his morning walk. Sara's Alzheimer's demanded a structure to their days, a predictable ebb and flow of time and activity, and the after-breakfast stroll, weather permitting, was a fixed item on their daily agenda. Her absence did not tempt him to slack off.

Most mornings, they walked a mile. She could go greater distances, but he fatigued easily and turned them back home before he lost his wind. Today's walk would be brief. He made his way along Falmouthport's main road at a steady pace, determined not to think about the day's agenda. He focused on happier times, thinking about David, Anne, and the boys, the many trips he and Sara had taken in the past, and his career highlights. However, as he neared the quarter-mile mark, memories of his precious daughter, Lisa, gone for almost twenty-seven years, intruded.

Too often lately, when he felt life closing in on him, felt his losses most keenly, he thought of Lisa. They'd lost her in a freak drowning accident off the shores of Corn Hill Beach, in Truro, on the outer reaches of Cape Cod. Once past the immediate trauma, Jack had buried his heartache deep inside, moving on with his life, excelling at his job, and buying and operating Blue Hydrangeas, trying to forget. It didn't work. Even now, he continued to suffer sleepless nights, thrashing in the sheets until he couldn't bear it any longer, and then slipping out of bed to pace through the dark house. He relived that terrible day, imagining all sorts of scenarios in which Lisa survived, before mercifully finding his way back to sleep, his dreams disconnected and frightening, full of loss and desolation. He'd awaken unrested and bleary-eyed.

The worst of it was that as his memories of Lisa's death grew more vivid, Sara seemed to have forgotten all about her. He'd tried to deny it, but an episode last February had forced him to admit that the Alzheimer's had erased Sara's memories of their daughter.

They were sitting on the sofa in their family room during a light snowfall. A fire burned in the fireplace and classical music played in the background. They passed the time poking around in a box of old photos taken in the 1970's at their summerhouse. Seeing them pained Jack, but he patiently sat by her side and listened to her ramble on with her recollections, even when they didn't make sense.

Sara, an amateur photographer, had chronicled her children's lives with an old 35-mm camera she'd picked up at a flea market. In the photos, David and Lisa were young teenagers, gangly, smiling, and full of life. Sara sorted through pictures of them playing on the beach, building sandcastles, flying kites. She rummaged aimlessly through the stacks of photos, but one in particular captivated her and she studied it for some time.

Lisa sat on the beach, her long auburn hair floating in the breeze, her bright eyes and glowing skin forever sixteen. She wore a flowered bikini. Her lanky legs were lean and tanned. Sara rifled through the pile of pictures but kept returning to this one. She laid it down and picked it up again several times, struggling to find the right words to express her thoughts. Her facial expressions changed rapidly, showing a spark of recognition, replaced by bewilderment, and then the thread was lost. She held the picture up to the light and spoke with trepidation.

"Do I know this girl?"

"Of course you know her—" he started to explain, but stopped, tripping over his words. He took the picture from her and cradled it in his palm, gazing at the girl who was once his greatest joy. He glanced up at the mantel over the fireplace where pictures of Lisa blended in with the family photos. Choked with emotion, he turned away to catch his breath and pondered how to respond. Had Sara forgotten this girl was their daughter? Had her illness robbed her of even this most treasured memory? It was unthinkable, unbearable. He debated telling her the truth, but, uncertain of her reaction, simply said, "She's a girl we used to know."

"At Corn Hill?" Sara asked, still staring at the picture.

"At Corn Hill," he replied. "We have lots of pictures of her, see?" He pointed to the photographs scattered across the table.

She gave no sign of recognition. A moment passed, and she yawned. "Put all this away." She rose from the sofa and stretched her arms high over her head. "I want to go to bed."

Jack left the photographs where they lay and escorted her upstairs to their bedroom. After tucking her in, he headed back down and gathered the pictures into neat piles, storing them in their boxes. His hands shook as the boxes filled.

He went to the mantel and removed the pictures of Lisa, hiding them away in a cabinet. Better to keep them out of sight in case Sara noticed them and started asking more questions, or, even worse, stumbled on the truth. A sudden revelation might be devastating, and he was determined to spare her any angst.

He turned out the light in the living room and made for the stairs, but, overcome with emotion, he dropped into an armchair and let out a strangled sob. The clock struck midnight as he mourned their daughter in isolation, crying in the dark for Lisa, his wife, and himself. Gone was any possibility they might speak of her, recalling the good times and special memories, or comfort one another as they grieved. It was as if she had never existed.

Jack sat up deep into the night, and wondered how much time remained before Sara forgot him as well.

Jack picked up his pace and dismissed his troublesome thoughts. Today was not a day for self-pity. He turned back before the half-mile mark, eager to return home. He had a few things on his to-do list before leaving for the hospital. Sara's flowerbeds needed watering before the summer heat got the best of them. He drenched the gardens and flowerpots, then deadheaded the petunias and picked out a few weeds. A mediocre gardener, he managed to keep it all alive. A professional landscaper did most of the heavy work, and Sara puttered around when she was up for it.

After caring for the flowers, Jack went in to the kitchen and put away the few dishes lying in the dish rack. There weren't many when the table was set for one.

Jack loathed being home alone. He found the silent house cold and lonely. He liked a house bustling with activity: a television or radio turned on somewhere, baked goods in the oven, visitors coming and going. With Sara away, Jack avoided staying home and found any excuse to be out: eating at restaurants, taking walks, and playing golf.

Before leaving for the hospital, he took a quick tour of the house, inspecting each room. First stop was the formal dining room, where they hadn't served a dinner other than a birthday or holiday celebration in years. The day before, Mrs. Wright had polished the antique table and chairs he and Sara had found ages ago at an estate sale in Chatham. The glass panels in the magnificent matching hutch were dust and fingerprint-free, no doubt from the housekeeper's impeccable attention to detail. The china in the hutch was a treasure Sara had discovered one winter in a second hand store in Sandwich. Such a find overjoyed her: a complete set for twelve. The room was ready for a party, but no one was coming.

He moved on to the formal living room, a favorite gathering place when Blue Hydrangeas was open for business. Their guests had used the room to unwind and socialize, and Sara had shown and sold much of her artwork there. They hadn't used it in years. Two large sofas and a couple of overstuffed armchairs encouraged visitors to stay awhile. A bookcase covered one long wall, overflowing with books. This room, too, appeared showcase-perfect, like a picture in *Better Homes and Gardens* or *House Beautiful.*

The family room was their private haven, off limits to guests. While Sara had her studio for peace and privacy, this room was Jack's domain. It had a sunken floor, fireplace, and home theater system. Large pieces of furniture invited all who entered to sprawl out on the cushions. Jack and Sara had spent many evenings cuddled on the worn but comfortable couch, watching TV or reading.

Climbing the stairs, he checked on the six bedrooms, one for David and Anne, two for Jesse and Derek, and the others for guests. Unique Cape Cod themes decorated each guestroom, giving it its own personality: the Dunes Room, the Lighthouse Room, the Marina Room, and the Garden Room. These rooms had been booked solid most summers, but for far too long no one other than David, Anne, and their boys had come to stay. Jack peeked into each room, noting they remained as he'd left them at yesterday's inspection. All they required was a light dusting and some vacuuming once a week from Mrs. Wright.

Satisfied all was in order, Jack finished his chores in plenty of time to make his ten o'clock appointment at the hospital. He let the cats in and locked up the house. Heading down the path leading from the front door to the driveway, he stopped to take a deep breath. Sara had planted a fragrant herb garden outside the door, thick with the soothing scent of lavender. It hugged the walkway along the side of the house.

Sara loved color and her gardens were full of it. Over the years, she'd planted thousands of seeds, plants, and bulbs, a fortune in dollars and energy spent. The color and glory of Sara's flowerbeds had no end.

At the front of the yard were her prizewinning roses, vibrant pink, in perfect, cascading buds spilling over a split rail fence. And just ahead of them, along each side of the winding driveway, bloomed her hydrangeas as blue as the summer sky. A dozen bushes, the Blue Prince variety, spread out on each side with lush foliage and fresh, delicate flowers. She'd planted them their first year in the house. With her tender care and some help from a green thumb, they'd flourished and made a sensational entrance to the front door.

As Jack strode toward his Lincoln, he gazed at the garden, pleased with its beauty. Then, just as he had done each day on his way to the hospital, he stopped at a hydrangea bush and selected one perfect flower. He cut it free with a pocketknife, carried it to the car, and placed it across the passenger seat. It was his gift to Sara, a piece of home, a reminder of better and easier times.

Chapter Eight

Jack didn't get far from Blue Hydrangeas before the chime of his cell phone pierced the car's silence. No stranger to technology, he had a love for better and faster digital conveniences. He bought a new computer every two or three years and was proud of his ability to navigate the Internet, depending on it to run the inn and keep up with the stock market, world news, and old friends. The cell phone, too, was a new necessity. How he wished he'd had it during his working days. What a difference that would have made. He pulled over and answered the call on the third ring.

"Dad, it's me," said David. "I had some car trouble and I'm going to be late." A late meeting the evening before had prevented him from spending the night at Blue Hydrangeas, and he'd assured his father he'd be at the hospital to handle any last minute arrangements. He planned to guide his parents through the admissions process, see his mother settled, and serve as a source of support, especially for Jack.

"What happened?" Jack asked, panic in his voice. "An accident?" Since Lisa's death, he worried something terrible might also happen to his son.

"No, nothing like that. I think it's the alternator. The car just died. I'm in Braintree." He was more than an hour away.

"Well, they expect us at ten. I'm on my way now." Jack glanced at the clock on the dashboard. He hated to be late for an appointment.

"Yeah, I know. A tow truck is coming. Anne's meeting me at the repair shop. As soon as she gets here, we'll be back on the road. Listen, Dad, wait for us at the hospital," he instructed. "Promise me you won't leave until we get there."

"Sure thing," Jack said. "Your mother will be glad to see you."

"Keep your phone turned on and with you," David ordered. Jack tended to leave the phone turned off or in the car. "I'll call you if we're going to be later than noon."

Jack agreed and continued on his way. Traffic on Route 28 frustrated him. No matter how long he lived in this popular vacation spot he would never grow accustomed to the summer traffic.

He arrived at the hospital ahead of schedule and headed up to the fourth floor where Sara had a private room. He found her sitting in a chair, drinking a glass of milk and eating graham crackers. She wore the white shorts and plaid blouse he'd brought for her the day before. Someone had woven her wavy, white hair into a French braid. Her skin had recovered its rosy glow. She was smiling at the young woman who sat with her. Jack recognized Verlaine and nodded to the young nursing assistant as he walked over to his wife.

"Well, here you are," he said, breaking into a broad smile.

Sara's face turned radiant. "Hello, darling," she answered.

"Ready to get out of here?" he asked, pleased to see her so alert.

"Good morning, Mr. Harmon," said Verlaine. "She's all set." She'd packed Sara's few belongings into an overnight bag.

Jack had packed a much larger suitcase at home the night before. Marlene, the Admissions Director at Bayside Village, had advised him to bring in a few personal items on the first day to help Sara feel more comfortable. Unsure of what to bring, he threw in a few nightgowns, socks and underwear, some shorts, long pants, a few blouses, and a couple of sweaters. He added her lavender shampoo and

111

the few cosmetics she used. At the last minute, he slipped in a sketchbook and a fresh box of pencils. The bag waited in the trunk of the car.

"She's having a great day," Verlaine went on. "We're sorry to see her go."

"I'm glad to go home," Sara declared, then, remembering her manners, added, "Although everyone here has been nice."

"How did you sleep, Sara? Did you make it through the night?" Jack asked.

"Well, of course I did, Jack. What a silly question."

Jack looked at Verlaine.

"She woke up around four," the nursing assistant said.

"The usual routine?" Jack asked.

Verlaine nodded. "She fell back to sleep around seven, and woke up about a half hour ago. The rest did her well. She's very alert this morning."

Sara watched them converse and said, "You two talk about me like I'm not even here."

"I'm sorry, Sara," Jack said. "I just wanted to hear what Verlaine had to say about it."

"I could have told you myself," Sara huffed.

"I know you could, honey. I won't do it again."

"I'll let the nurse know you're here," Verlaine said.

"Are we going right home?" Sara asked, watching Verlaine leave the room.

Jack sat in the chair facing her and searched her face, desperate for any sign she remembered their plans. He couldn't tell. He sighed, resigned to explain it all over again.

"Sara, you know we're not going right home. We talked about it yesterday. Dr. Fallon thinks you need to go somewhere for a while to build up your strength, and I agree. When you're better, I can take you home."

"Why can't I go home today?" she said, indignant. "I'm fine, really. I want to go home," she demanded, a spark of trouble in her eyes.

Jack gazed out the window and avoided her stare. He'd dreaded this moment, and prayed she'd go along with him without questions. What a foolish idea. Sara didn't go along with anything unless she knew exactly what was happening. He made a silent promise to visit her every day, to call her every evening to say good night. He vowed to sit with her and the photo albums for as long as she wanted, to listen to her ramble on with her memories and not correct her.

Still, it wouldn't be enough. None of it would fill the aching void inside of him, or erase the guilt of his betrayal. He had made this plan with David and Dr. Fallon in Sara's best interest, but it was not her plan. No one had asked her what she wanted. He knew, given the choice, she would not have made the wisest one, but he also knew, deep down inside, that what we all want in the end is to go home.

A nurse entered the room carrying a paper medicine cup containing Sara's morning pills. Julie had a gentle way about her and a load of patience. She had a special spot in her heart for Sara, and sometimes brought her a big cup of coffee and the jelly donuts she loved. Jack appreciated such loving gestures.

"Here you go, Sara," Julie said, offering her the medicine cup. She poured her a cup of water and handed it to her. Sara took the pills and put them in her mouth, then reached for the cup of water, took a sip, and swallowed the medicine. She opened her mouth and Julie checked that the pills were gone.

"Good," said Julie, turning to Jack. "How are you, Mr. Harmon? You look great. Your brief respite seems to have done wonders."

"I'm feeling pretty good today, Julie," Jack said.

"Then that makes two of you. Sara is doing so much better. She's steadier on her feet, and has even been walking around the unit unassisted."

"That's good to hear," Jack said.

"Really," Sara said, "what's the big deal? Anyone can walk around this place. You just go round and round in a big circle. There's nothing to it."

"You couldn't get out of bed a few days ago," Jack reminded her.

"I don't see what all the fuss is about. I'm perfectly fine," she said.

"Yes, you are," Julie said. "And you're all packed and ready to go. They're expecting you at Bayside Village by eleven."

"Bayside Village?" Sara stiffened, her expression guarded. "Why are we going there?"

Jack and the nurse glanced at each other. Julie took her cue. They'd spoken by phone earlier that morning about what to expect when it came time for Sara to leave the hospital. She'd told him sending a patient off to a place like Bayside Village had its difficulties. A woman like Sara, confused, but not all of the time, wouldn't understand why she was going there. Julie assured Jack she'd handled situations like this for years. She spoke up now, her tender voice easing the tension.

"Sara, you've been unwell and you're just starting to get back on your feet. Jack hasn't been well either, remember? He hurt his back, and he needs some time to get into better shape, too. He and your son, and Dr. Fallon, want you to stay at Bayside Village for a while to get your strength back. People go there all the time. I'm sure you'll like it."

"Like it?" Sara asked, fire in her eyes. "What's to like about it?" She turned to Jack. "Are you trying to get rid of me?"

Jack paled. "No way," he said. "This is only a temporary thing, just a week, so you can recuperate."

"You're being silly, Jack. I can recuperate at home." She clutched at the buttons on her blouse, twisting and turning them.

Jack glanced hopelessly at Julie.

"It'll be so much better at Bayside Village," Julie reassured Sara. "You'll get physical therapy every day to make you strong. You know how much you enjoy that. And, they have all kinds of activities and plenty of things to do. You'll meet new friends. You might even know some of the people who are already there."

"Why would I know anyone there?" Sara asked, pulling at the buttons until one dangled by a thread. "I don't even know where it is."

"Of course you know where it is," Jack said. "We went there many times to visit Rose's mother, remember?"

"That place?" Sara huffed. "Well, I can't see why I would be going there. Doesn't seem like some place I would want to go to."

"It's a short stay," Jack said, growing weary of this resistance, although it was what he had expected. "Just a few days and then I'll bring you home."

"Where are you going to be?" She'd stopped pulling at the buttons and dropped her hands in her lap, knitting her fingers together.

"I'll be at home, waiting for you."

"Alone?"

"I can manage," he said. "Besides, I'll visit you every day." Jack reached for her hand and squeezed it. "We'll go out, if you'd like, to lunch, or supper, or shopping. We'll go to the movies. It'll be like going on a date."

Sara turned from one to the other. Jack held his breath, braced for another objection. At last, she smiled. "As long as you promise to come and see me every day," she told him with a wink. "I'd like that."

Jack covered her hands with both of his. "I'll be there," he promised.

Julie breathed a sigh of relief. "The paperwork's out at the desk," she told Jack. "I'll ask Verlaine to find a wheelchair, and if you'll carry the suitcase she'll wheel Mrs. Harmon out."

"Julie, I can't thank you enough for all of your help," Jack said as she turned to leave.

She stopped in the doorway and smiled back at him. "You have no need to thank me, Mr. Harmon. Sara's as sharp as a razor today. This stay has done her well. Take care." She hurried out of the room.

Minutes later Verlaine entered with a wheelchair and helped Sara into it. Jack picked up her bag. They wheeled her down to the lobby and he went to retrieve the car. Verlaine helped him move Sara into the Lincoln's front seat.

"Jack, how lovely," Sara said when she spotted the hydrangea bloom wilting in the late morning sun. She moved the flower to the console between their seats, out of the heat.

Jack settled into the driver's seat, waved goodbye to Verlaine, and pulled out of the hospital parking lot. Bayside Village was just fifteen minutes away. He drove with great care, making small talk about the weather, his golf game, anything except where they were going or why.

"I played a foursome with Stan, Joe Miller, and Harry Scott yesterday," he told her. "Stan and I beat the pants off them."

"Of course you did," she said. "You and Stan are champs." Jack and Stan had taken turns as club champion for years, competing against one another with a fierce but friendly rivalry, and reigning over everyone when they paired together as a team. It had been many years since either of them had brought home a trophy.

"By the way," Jack said, "I saw Stan and Rose this morning. They said they'd come see you soon. Emily called, too. She and Ed will be up for a visit in a week or two."

"That's nice." They drove in silence for a few minutes. When they passed a home with a flourishing display of wildflowers, she asked, "How's my garden? Is it still there?"

He laughed and shook his head. "I haven't been head gardener that long," he answered. "It's fine. I watered everything just before I left the house." While Sara had a pepper green thumb, Jack's was as brown as a potato. It was their experience that if she left him alone with

118

the garden long enough he'd soon turn it dry and lifeless.

"Good," she said, "I'd hate to lose it all this early in the season."

Verlaine and Julie were right, he thought. *Sara* is *having a good day, a great day.* It had been weeks since her mind was this clear. He couldn't remember the last time they'd had such an enjoyable conversation.

Dr. Fallon had once explained that after a hospital stay Sara was in prime condition, free of infection, well-nourished, well-hydrated, with stable vital signs and normal blood counts. She was alert and oriented and had more energy and higher functioning. He credited this to the twenty-four-hour nursing care she received while in the hospital. The nurses alerted him immediately to any deviation in her medical status and he corrected it at once. The physical therapists worked with her daily to build up her strength. The nurses and their assistants met all of her needs non-stop, around the clock.

This twenty-four hour care and attention made a tremendous impact on her physical and mental well-being. However, once back at home, with Jack alone to provide this care, her condition slowly deteriorated. By the time he suspected something was wrong, it had gone too far, and required acute medical intervention.

Dr. Fallon had also explained that at Bayside Village, as in the hospital, the nursing staff would observe Sara twenty-four hours a day and correct any fluctuations in her condition as they occurred. She would remain stable, and she and Jack would have many more good days. Theoretically, Jack followed this logic, but he was heartbroken when he thought of the loss of her presence in his life in so many crucial ways.

No more waking up beside her every morning.

No more eating ice cream out on the deck after supper.

No more staying up late at night, cuddled on the couch, watching the old movies they loved.

They'd live separately, apart from each other, like in their courtship days when he lived on the road as a pharmaceuticals salesman while she attended art school in Manhattan. They saw each other at prearranged times and had little privacy. The young ladies residing in Sara's dormitory followed rigid rules and adhered to a strict curfew. The housemother observed visits with male callers in the common room. Maintaining any intimacy was impossible. Jack mourned the loss of that intimacy now. Things were about to change, and he didn't welcome it.

As they cut their way through the gnarly traffic on Route 28, he pointed out different sights along the way: a mini mall under construction at a busy intersection, a stray cat prancing along the road, another couple passing them in a car just like theirs. Soon they came upon Cap'n Bill's Seafood Shanty.

"There's Cap'n Bill's." Jack stopped for a red light. "You hungry?"

"Some fried scallops sound good right about now," she replied.

He noted it was almost eleven, made the right turn into the parking lot, and parked. They'd have lunch together before checking into Bayside Village.

They settled into a booth at the rear of the restaurant, a small spot with a half dozen booths and a long counter lined with worn leather stools. Lobster traps filled with plastic seaweed, lobsters, and crabs hung from the ceiling. Mounted on the wall over the take-out counter was an old ship's wheel. Buoys of all colors, most of them worn pale by the sea, were strung all over. The menu offered a variety of fresh seafood. Sara preferred the scallops, deep-fried, with French fries, coleslaw, and tartar sauce on the side. She ordered it every time. Jack, ever mindful of his diet, played it safe and ordered broiled cod fish with a baked potato and a side salad dressed with oil and vinegar.

They sat in comfortable silence while waiting for their food, lost in their own thoughts. They'd sat in this restaurant many times. Jack wondered how many more of these times lay ahead. The idea of taking Sara out whenever, wherever he wanted to was wonderful, but in all likelihood it probably sounded a lot easier than it was.

"How did we ever find this place?" she asked. She picked at her napkin, caught herself fidgeting, and folded her arms.

"We knew the original owners," Jack answered, thinking back. The owners had been summer time neighbors in the Corn Hill days.

"I think I remember them from when we used to stay in Truro," she mused.

Warning bells went off in Jack's head. Talk of Truro had become frequent over the last few weeks, a dangerous topic.

For many summers, long before they'd bought Blue Hydrangeas and become full-time Cape Cod residents, they'd rented their favorite beach house in Truro, a town on the outer Cape situated just before Provincetown. While Sara derived great joy from her memories of Truro, Jack avoided or changed the subject whenever it came up. The horrible memory of Lisa's death lay buried beneath all of the happy memories encompassing Truro and the house near Corn Hill Beach. Sara hadn't mentioned Lisa in months, and he feared what might happen if she stumbled upon the loss of their daughter in her fragile condition. On this day in particular, he wanted to dodge any sudden revelations.

"Morrison, Bill and Jane Morrison." He answered her question and changed the subject. "You know, speaking of them reminds me of the North Shore, that's where they came from, remember? I ran into an old friend of mine from up there the other day, over at the golf club." He steered her away from memories buried in the back of her mind about times in Truro and told her about the conversation with his old friend.

They ate their lunch, Jack paid the bill, and they continued on their way to Bayside Village. Sara relaxed against the car's leather upholstery. They drove with the windows down, the gentle wind blowing the few stray hairs that had escaped from her French braid around her face. The sky was a clear blue, no clouds for miles ahead. Although the temperature had climbed to eighty-one degrees, a gentle breeze stirred the air. They traveled along the road leading to Bayside Village at a steady pace. Anyone observing them would have thought they were a content, elderly couple out for a relaxing drive.

Jack proceeded with caution, never one to speed. Sara was the one with the lead foot, although she hadn't driven in years. They'd talked about it only once, that awful morning when Sara went missing, the car was gone, and he was out of his mind with worry. She'd returned safe, but the events of that morning had distressed her unlike any other incident thus far in her disease. He'd helped her retrace her steps and together they pieced together her story. Shaken to the core by the morning's revelations, they agreed never to discuss it again, but Jack remembered the day she stopped driving as though it had happened yesterday.

Chapter Nine

Summer again, mid-August, and they had a house full of guests. Shortly after dawn, Sara let the cats out and headed for the kitchen. She pulled mixing bowls, canisters of flour and sugar, and a few spice jars from the cabinets. She gathered milk, eggs, butter, and fresh blueberries from the refrigerator, mixed the batter for the blueberry scones, filled the baking sheet, and slid it into the preheated oven. The radio, tuned to the local station, kept her in touch with Cape news and the weather report.

While the scones baked, she whipped up a batch of apple cinnamon muffins and prepared the batter for buttermilk pancakes. She filled the coffee pots with the house's special blend, and then poked through the refrigerator for the carton of cream she'd picked up at the supermarket the night before.

"Wait a minute," she mumbled under her breath, arranging and rearranging the items on each shelf. She pulled out cartons of milk and orange juice before finding a half-filled container of cream, not nearly enough for that morning's crowd.

"Darn it," she muttered, closing the refrigerator door. She checked the clock: almost seven. Most of their guests were still asleep, but noises from upstairs suggested one or two had come around to the promise of a summer day by the sea. The inn was booked, and they'd stayed up late into the night talking with their guests as if they'd known each other for years.

She was certain she had time for a quick trip to the Falmouthport Market before anyone came downstairs in search of breakfast. She double-checked the oven to make sure she'd turned it off and left nothing inside. She found her purse in the hall closet and tiptoed out of the house, careful to close the door behind her without a sound.

Outside, the air was warm and fragrant. Her Mercedes was waiting with the top down and she scolded herself, grateful no rain had fallen. The last time she'd let that happen Jack had been furious. It took days for the carpeting to dry out, and even now a musty odor emanated from the vehicle in humid weather.

The 1977 450 SL was a gift from Jack after they'd moved to the Cape and he joined the golf club. He'd teamed up with a man who owned a Mercedes dealership in Boston, and afterward he talked Jack into test-driving the shiny, red convertible. They took a spin through town, cruising through Falmouth Heights and along the shoreline. Jack fell in love with the car and bought it that day. Sara took one look at it as he cruised up the driveway and claimed it for herself. Jack tried to convince her she was better off with his old Town Car, but she was undeterred. Laughing and throwing his hands up, he caved in and handed her the keys.

"As long as you let me drive it on weekends," he bargained, and she agreed. She was known around town for the Mercedes, dashing from place to place, shopping for Blue Hydrangeas, attending town meetings and social events, and setting up her easel at the beach.

She settled into the convertible and the engine purred to life. The Falmouthport Market was a mile away and she planned to run in, buy the cream, and be back at Blue Hydrangeas before anyone missed her, twenty minutes tops.

At the end of the inn's winding driveway she turned left. At the second intersection, she took another left, then a right, and left again. She drove for several minutes before stopping at another intersection.

"Old Harbor Road and Station Avenue." She read the street signs aloud. "Hold on," she said, puzzled. "Station Avenue? This isn't the right place." She turned the car around and headed back along Old Harbor.

"I must have taken a wrong turn," she grumbled, and continued on her way. She glanced at the clock and gasped. Half past seven! Thirty minutes had passed and she hadn't even made it to the store. Jack was sure to be up by now, wondering what had happened to her.

She drove forward, the Mercedes hugging the side of the road. Her head swiveled back and forth, as she read the street signs aloud. Everything seemed unfamiliar. She had no idea where she was. Good Lord, it was happening again. Her heart raced. Her temples pounded. There was a terrible noise in her head and she realized it was the sound of her own keening voice.

She pulled over to the side of the road and stopped, cradling her head in her hands. She practiced the deep breathing exercises Dr. Fallon had taught her for times like this. It calmed her for a moment and her mind cleared. She sat in the car, watching the morning traffic buzz by.

"Calm down, Sara," she ordered. "You're not too far from home. Think, Sara, think." She tapped the left side of her head with an index finger. "You're on Old Harbor Road. Now, where is that and where does it go?"

She tried to draw a map in her head, to find her way mentally, but she couldn't think. Her thoughts were a jumbled mess and she couldn't make sense of any of them. She rubbed her eyes and found her hand wet with tears.

She was lost, and not for the first time. She'd been having problems with the car for months—near accidents, losing her way, driving around in circles. Jack had warned her about going out in the car alone, but she hadn't listened, hadn't wanted to listen. The Mercedes was her last link to freedom. If she gave that up, she'd be totally dependent on him. Eventually, she found her way back home and kept her troubles to herself.

The clock ticked away the minutes, taunting her, reminding her she'd been gone for more than an hour and Jack and her guests were back at the house unable to fix their coffee and wondering where she was.

She sucked in a deep breath, launched the car into drive, and swung into the road. The screech of brakes startled her. A pickup truck swerved around the Mercedes and cut her off, its horn blasting. An angry face poked out of the window.

"What are you, crazy? Get out of the road, you old bat," the driver shouted, waving his fist. The truck roared off with tires squealing.

Sara slammed on the brakes and moved out of the road. She glanced into the rear view mirror. Tire tracks marked the pavement behind her.

"My God," she cried. The truck had almost hit her.

Another vehicle pulled up behind her. A figure approached the Mercedes with caution and Sara tensed, afraid of the advancing stranger. A young woman in cutoff jeans and a T-shirt stuck her head in the window. She pushed her long, straight hair behind her ear.

"Are you okay?" she asked in a delicate voice.

Sara stared at her savior and gathered herself together. "I'm lost," she explained. "I'm trying to find a bed and breakfast. We call it Blue Hydrangeas. Do you know where it is?"

"I'm not from around here," the girl explained. "I'm only here for the summer. Do you know what street it's on?"

"It's on Starboard Road. In Falmouthport," Sara answered, brightening now that she had someone to talk to and her thinking had cleared.

"Well, Falmouthport's a few miles from here. Follow me. I'll take you to the turnoff. Can you find your way to the inn from there?"

Sara nodded and the girl returned to her car. Her beat-up Chevy pulled up beside the

Mercedes. The girl motioned for her to follow and Sara drove away from the scene of the near accident, away from Old Harbor Road, away from her confusion and meltdown.

The sight of familiar territory was a relief. At the entrance to Falmouthport, the Chevy stopped and Sara pulled up beside it.

"You okay, now?" The girl leaned out of the window.

"I think so," Sara said. "Thank you. You're a nice girl, and a good person, to help a stranger."

The girl blushed and brushed away the compliment. "No problem," she muttered. "Take care now." The Chevy sped away.

Sara reached Blue Hydrangeas just before eight-thirty. She entered the kitchen through the slider off the deck, hoping to avoid running into anyone until she'd freshened up.

Jack confronted her as soon as she came in. "Where have you been? I've been out of my mind with worry. You know you're not supposed to go out in the car without me."

A steady chatter flowed from the dining room, punctuated with bursts of laughter and the clink of silver against china.

"I went to get cream," Sara answered, sidestepping him.

"Why? Didn't we buy it last night?" He blocked her path.

"I thought we did, but I couldn't find it this morning." She avoided looking at him.

"Then where's the cream you just bought?"

Empty-handed, she stared at the floor and shook her head. "I didn't buy it. I guess I forgot." She squeezed past him to escape up the back stairs.

"How could you forget it?" He began following her up the stairs. "Sara, what is going on with you?"

"Forget it, Jack," she shouted before slamming the bedroom door behind her.

He prepared to go up after her but paused when he heard footsteps behind him. He turned and looked down at Roy Pearson, the businessman from Ohio visiting for the week with his wife, a voluptuous blonde less than half his age. The walleyed guest stood at the bottom of the stairs staring up at him.

Jack descended the stairs and switched from anxious husband to gracious host. "Can I help you, Roy?"

"You've run out of cream."

"Yes, I've heard that," Jack said, "although I'm sure we bought a big carton last night." He rummaged through the refrigerator and, not finding the cream, pulled out a carton of whole milk instead.

"I'm sorry," he said, "but I guess I was wrong. We seem to have run out of cream. I'll order some, but in the meantime you can try this."

"Sure," said Roy. "That's what I use at home anyway."

"Please have a seat and I'll bring it right in," Jack said, dismissing him. He opened a kitchen cabinet to find a pitcher for the cream and stopped short. A half-gallon of light cream sat on a shelf at room temperature. Sara must have put it there instead of in the refrigerator when she unloaded the groceries. He sagged against the counter, his head resting on the cabinet's lower edge. "Patience, Jack," he reminded himself. "She didn't mean it."

He composed himself and disposed of the ruined cream. He poured milk into a crystal pitcher, brought it into the dining room, and placed it on the table in front of the Pearsons.

Jack went back to the kitchen and called the Falmouthport Market. "Have Jimmy bring over a couple of quarts of light cream, okay? And some half-and-half." Jimmy was good. He'd deliver in a few minutes and earn a nice tip.

After checking on his guests, Jack headed upstairs and found Sara on the chaise in their bedroom practicing her deep breathing exercises, her eyes closed. The lids were pink and puffy and he knew she'd been crying. She looked beat, her face pale, her skin damp. Tiny tendrils of fuzzy white hair stuck out from the chignon piled up high on her head. She absentmindedly stroked Cleo, who lay stretched out and purring on her lap.

Jack patiently waited for her to tell him what was wrong. She turned to him mournfully, her lips trembling.

"I went to the market to get the cream," she explained, her voice strained. She took some deep breaths and started over, more composed, her voice stronger. "I got lost." She told him the whole story, what she remembered of it.

The sound of chairs pushing away from the dining room table strayed upstairs. Breakfast was over and their guests carried on with the day. He checked the clock – ten minutes before nine.

"I was gone a long time, wasn't I?" she asked.

"I don't know what time you left," he answered.

"I left before seven. I was gone for more than an hour, and the market is less than ten minutes away." She stroked the cat's soft fur, a persistent motion that grounded her. Here in the safety and comfort of her bedroom she recovered from the morning's stress. "And Jack, don't get mad, but I almost had an accident."

"My God, Sara, are you all right? Did somebody hit you?"

"I said I *almost* had an accident. I'm fine and the car's fine. Anyway, I was so scared, and so mixed up. I can't explain it. I thought a few minutes went by, but when I looked at the clock, I saw it was late, and I didn't know where I was. I couldn't think straight."

"Why didn't you call me? You know that's why I bought you the cell phone." He looked toward her dresser where the phone lay plugged into its charger.

"If not for that girl, I'd probably still be there, still lost," Sara mused. The ordeal over, her voice was as calm as the breeze fluttering through the window.

Jack shook his head. "Honey," he said, "we've talked about your driving before. You know your reflexes aren't sharp and your sense of direction is not what it used to be. These periods of confusion, of being 'mixed up,' are happening more often. I'm afraid something terrible will happen."

Sara stared out the window, refusing to look at him. "We're not going to beat this, are we?" she murmured.

Jack pretended not to hear her and focused on their immediate problem. "Please, Sara, don't get upset," he pleaded, "but we need to rethink your driving. You shouldn't go off on your own. I'll take you where you need to go."

Sara patted the cat, refusing to respond. Tears pooled in her eyes and she defiantly brushed them away.

"We have to be responsible. We can't risk an accident. I don't want anything to happen to you. And, I don't want anything to happen to anyone else. Think of that, Sara. You could hurt someone else."

His words sounded like knives to his own ears and he saw her flinch with each point he made. Her tears were heartbreaking, and he went to her, kneeled at her feet, and held her in his arms.

"I'm sorry, honey, but you know it's for the best."

Sara went on stroking the cat and said nothing. She handed over the keys to the Mercedes without looking at him.

After a few moments, Jack returned to their guests and saw them off on their day's adventures with tips on where to have lunch and the best beaches in the area. When they'd gone he cleaned up the kitchen and dining room, working quietly, making things just so as he prepared for their return later on. They'd be thirsty and looking for Sara's sun-brewed iced tea and the homemade oatmeal cookies she set out for them each afternoon.

Sara remained upstairs, and he missed her help and her presence as he set the tea to brew out on the deck, although he knew it was best that she stay by herself while she absorbed this latest indignity.

This morning's episode finally convinced him that running the bed and breakfast was too much for them. Over the years, they'd developed a routine, a system that worked and allowed them to operate the inn efficiently. Jack handled the business side of things, managing the money and marketing, maintaining the website and reservations system, and working with the advertisers and the innkeeper's association. Sara managed the kitchen and guestrooms with the help of Mrs. Wright. Together they created menus, shopped for supplies, did the cooking and baking, and supervised the housekeeping help. However, as Sara's Alzheimer's advanced, they had to alter their routine, and little by little, Jack took on some of Sara's duties in addition to his own.

Sara had always risen before dawn to start breakfast, and when Jack came downstairs in the morning the kitchen smelled delicious. Now, he rose with her and joined her in the kitchen, subtly supervising her work as she put on the coffee and set out the homemade baked goods, fresh fruit, and other breakfast items. He didn't mind helping her with prep and cleanup, but the hustle and bustle of waiting on people and feeding them was tiresome. He preferred to visit with their guests and help them plan their day while Sara saw that everyone was well fed and happy. He told them where to find the best lobster dinner and gave instructions on how to catch the ferries to Nantucket and Martha's Vineyard. Fortunately, Sara loved playing hostess, and most days handled it like a pro, on autopilot, barely breaking a sweat.

She also had her dark days, when she was so tired she couldn't climb out of bed, and Jack took over, rushing to the bakery to buy pastries, bagels, and rolls, and brewing pot after pot of coffee. He set the table, laid out the jams and jellies, butter and cream cheese, and poured milk and orange juice. He waited on their guests reluctantly, but with a smile on his face, never letting on that anything was wrong. When breakfast was over, he cleaned it all up.

He was too old to shoulder all of this responsibility by himself, and Sara was too unreliable, too prone to getting mixed up, making mistakes and causing him increased work. Yet, even on her darkest day, she had never disappeared, and he feared this new twist in her illness made running the bed and breakfast impossible. He couldn't take care of Sara and manage the inn, too.

When Labor Day passed and the last of their guests had checked out, Jack closed the front door behind them for good.

Chapter Ten

Jack gazed at Sara sitting beside him in the passenger seat, her eyes closed. Her face wore no expression, no hint of worry. She could have been sleeping. After she had given him the keys to the Mercedes, she never once asked if she could drive, but sometimes he'd catch her eyeing his hands on the steering wheel or watching his foot on the brake and he knew she wanted to be in the driver's seat herself. But, as time went on she forgot about driving, and he was grateful that the forgetting made it easier for her to bear her loss. Jack reached over and caressed her hand. Without opening her eyes, she took grasp of his hand and gave it a warm squeeze.

As they approached the road to Bayside Village, Jack's heart rate began to accelerate and the familiar ache started in his chest. He fumbled in his pocket for the small vial of nitroglycerin tablets. The familiar feel of the tiny glass bottle comforted him.

A huge signpost announced the turnoff. Blue lettering on a white background proclaimed, "Bayside Village: A Senior Residential Community." A drawing of a wave curling toward shore embellished the elegant sign. An arrow pointed to a fork in the road leading to the complex of condominiums, senior housing, and nursing facility. Jack slowed down, prepared to take the turn, and glanced at Sara. She was wide-awake and gazing at the expanse of green lawn and vibrant gardens dotting the landscape, a curious expression on her face.

"Bayside Village," she read. "What is this place?"

"This is it. This is where you'll be staying for the next week," Jack answered.

He drove up the long entranceway leading to the assisted living center. It was beautiful, the grounds well maintained. Built on a bluff, the complex had a magnificent view of the ocean. On the way up the drive, he caught glimpses of whitecaps. The golf course was on his left and he saw several people strolling across the green or riding through in golf carts. The condominiums stood on the other side of the golf course, high on a hill, white and pristine in the afternoon sun. He pointed it all out to Sara, who nodded and added her own comments.

"Oh, Jack, look at the hydrangeas." She pointed to a mass of the white mop head flowers. "Annabelle's," she declared. "That color is exquisite, and they're so big."

"Almost as nice as yours," Jack teased with a wink.

"Almost," she said, and winked back.

The assisted living center stood on the far right of the complex. Jack followed the road to where it turned and saw it, a replica of a Queen Anne Victorian, and three stories high, with sprawling additions on either side and to the rear. During his working years, Jack had visited many such facilities throughout the northeast, but this was unlike any other he had seen. Most appeared cold, clinical, and institutional, but he had to admit Bayside Village seemed warm and welcoming, more like somebody's home than a health care facility.

True to Cape Cod style, clapboard covered the front and the rest of the building was sided with weathered cedar shingles. The trim was white, the shutters a pale green. A wraparound porch encircled the front and each side. The residents' rooms were in the left and right wings, and the dining room, activity areas, visitor's center and administrative offices were located in the middle.

A circular drive made its way to the front, similar to the one at Jack and Sara's home, but bordered by a perennial garden that rivaled Blue Hydrangeas': Echinacea, Dahlias, snap dragons, lady slipper, calendula. The beautiful gardens reassured him. During his initial visit, he'd learned the residents worked in the gardens and did most of the planting and weeding, which would be good therapy for Sara. He noted all of this to her as they came around the drive and stopped in front of the building.

The tinkle of wind chimes filled the air. A few people moved in and out of the main entrance, watched by several others who sat on the front porch in wheelchairs. They were a sad group. Many wore knitted shawls in the July heat. Jack watched a man shuffle back and forth, from one end of the porch to the other, mumbling to himself. A blue-haired woman sat in a wheelchair crying soundlessly, her gnarled fingers working a string of rosary beads. A frail, shriveled woman slept in a recliner, snoring, her mouth wide open. Jack remembered Marlene, the redheaded Admissions Director, telling him and Rose that most of the residents were active and fully functioning. Distracted with his own thoughts and worries during their visit, he hadn't noticed anyone at all. The sight of these people dismayed him.

Sara stared out of the window, wordless. *What is she thinking?* he wondered. He prepared himself for another vehement outburst, an adamant refusal to go inside. He wouldn't blame her for being angry with him for bringing her here. But, when she spoke, it was with resignation and in a brittle voice that made her sound very old.

"You want me to stay here with these people?"

His heart broke at the sight of her, eyes glossy with tears as the reality of the situation dawned on her. The space between them stretched a thousand miles. Never had he felt so far away from her, so helpless and impotent. He knew that once they crossed that front porch they would be living separate lives, married but not part of the intimacy and intricacy of each other's days. The Alzheimer's had won. Inside that building, the future was bleak. Outside, in the bright afternoon sun, the day spread before them with infinite possibilities.

His attention returned to the people huddled on the porch. They looked so lost and hopeless. *We're not ready for this,* he thought.

He put the car in drive and began easing it away from the building. Sara wouldn't be checking into Bayside Village today.

"Where are we going?" she asked, turning around in her seat to look back at the people on the porch.

"We're going for a ride," he said. He flipped the switch on his cell phone to "off," and cruised down the driveway.

Chapter Eleven

With the dishes done and not much else on her agenda, Rose Fantagucci took a paperback novel out to her chaise lounge by the pool and parked herself for a sun soaking and a good story. A lover of romance novels, she'd read hundreds and never grew bored. This one was particularly steamy, and she was nearing its predictable happy ending. She couldn't think of a better way to idle away her morning. Stan had taken off with their youngest grandson for some fishing and a picnic, and she had the whole house to herself.

Midway through her reading she paused, troubled by thoughts of Sara and her move to Bayside Village. Rose had no sisters, and over the years, Sara had almost become one. Oh, how she missed her friend. They'd spent a lot of time together, both with and without their husbands, but the Alzheimer's had changed everything, and although she'd been through this before, Rose had a hard time accepting it.

She'd surmised long ago that Jack was losing his grip on things, but she was afraid to bring up the subject with him because she didn't want to call in to question his ability to care for his wife. Any criticism of his caregiving, any suggestion that Sara might be better off with people specially trained to care for those with Alzheimer's, raised his hackles. It could be very unpleasant.

Besides, what did she know? She could be wrong, and some quality time with Sara at home still lay ahead. She debated the subject with herself and with Stan frequently, hoping for the best, but that chance encounter with Sara this past spring had convinced her that Sara and Jack were at a major turning point.

Memorial Day had passed, and the midmorning air was warm and fragrant with the scent of lilacs. Rose was an early riser, a trait that made her a successful innkeeper. An excellent cook, her kitchen hummed before dawn with breakfast preparations for family members and friends staying at the house. After cleaning up and straightening out the dining room, she moved on to her next favorite activity and stepped outdoors to attend to her garden. Like Blue Hydrangeas, Sea Song boasted immaculate grounds and flowers bloomed everywhere. A wildflower garden covered a quarter acre on the west side of the house. An eclectic assortment of outdoor furniture dotted the lawn.

The privet hedges at the foot of the drive begged for a trim and she headed for them with a stepladder and clippers in hand. She inhaled the late spring air, enjoying it since she'd quit smoking years ago, and set the ladder by the hedges. She clipped branches with fervor, engrossed in the task, stopping only to brush away the perspiration running down the back of her neck. Catching her breath, she noticed a familiar figure walking toward her. Shielding her eyes from the sun, she confirmed it was Sara, unaccompanied, and climbed down the ladder. *Where's Jack?* she wondered. He never let Sara walk alone. It had reached the point where she often lost her way, putting all of them through some serious stress until they found her. Rushing to meet her at the end of the drive, Rose greeted her with a big smile that belied her concern.

"My, you're out early," she said, taking her by the hand.

Sara acted surprised to see her. "Rose? What are you doing here?"

"I'm clipping the hedges. It's a glorious morning, and I figured I'd get out here and take care of them," Rose explained. She studied her friend, noting an uncertainty in her eyes that gave away her disorientation. Sara hid her confusion well, but Rose had a lot of experience with that—she'd cared for her own mother for fourteen years. "It's about time for a break. Would you like to come in for some lemonade? I made it this morning." She offered her hand and Sara gratefully latched onto it.

As they moved away from the road, Rose watched Sara study her surroundings with skepticism. A hand carved sign hung at the entrance to the drive. The white script on its blue background read, "Sea Song." It swayed in the breeze, creaking on its hinges. Sara stared at it, muttering the words.

"I must have taken a wrong turn," she said at last.

"No," replied Rose. "You're right where you need to be."

They strolled up the drive, Sea Song coming into view in its entire splendor. It was a magnificent sight, an original sea captain's house built in the nineteenth century. Stan and Rose had fallen in love with its Victorian charm and bought it as a foreclosure. People said they were crazy— better to tear it down and start fresh. They hadn't agreed, and spent years restoring and refurbishing it back to it original grandeur. Once their children had gone off to start their own families they rented out their rooms to Cape travelers. Rose enjoyed caring for her guests, and Stan delighted in meeting new people.

Their granddaughter and some of her friends were visiting for a few days. Relaxed and pampered bodies filled the rockers and wicker chairs on the porch. Empty coffee cups, crumb-littered breakfast plates, and newspapers lay strewn about the floor. Rose exchanged pleasantries with her guests as she and Sara made their way into the house.

"Where's Jack?" she casually asked as she and Sara entered the kitchen.

Sara gave her a blank stare, as though a veil had dropped over her eyes, and said, "Home, I guess." A puzzled expression followed a halfhearted smile.

Rose's heart sank. *Good Lord,* she thought, *it's happening again, and she'd been doing so well these last few weeks.* "Does he know you've gone walking?" she asked, pulling a hand-painted glass pitcher out of the refrigerator.

Sara stared at the fresh-cut lemon slices floating in the lemonade. "I don't know," she replied.

Rose poured two glasses and handed one to Sara. She accepted it with a trembling hand.

Rose sensed Sara's unease. Reluctant to embarrass her by exposing her confusion, she asked, "Why don't I call him and tell him you're here? I'll invite him over for some lemonade."

Jack picked up on the first ring.

"Thank God, Rose," he exclaimed when he learned Sara had wandered over to Sea Song.

"She slipped out while I was doing laundry. I never heard her leave. Is she all right?" Once assured that Sara was okay, he accepted her invitation to join them.

Rose brought Sara out to the back patio to wait for Jack. They sipped their lemonade in silence. Over the years, they'd spent many hours sitting together, at ease with one another, with no need for idle conversation to fill the silence. Rose observed Sara over the rim of her glass and noted she looked thin. Her skin stretched dry and tight across her face. Her hair hung loose and limp, crying out for a shampoo. She clung to an old corduroy blazer she'd wrapped around herself. Her hands were rough, the nails chipped and cracked. A beat-up pair of garden sneakers encased her tiny feet. How Rose envied those feet. Sara was petite and dainty, like a ballerina in a music box. Rose was tall and gawky, all clumsy angles and size ten feet with painful bunions that made it terribly difficult to find a good pair of shoes. Growing up, the other kids had tormented her with the nickname, "Olive Oyl."

She'd always thought Sara was perfect, put together by a loving Creator with patience and meticulous attention to detail. Now, as she examined her sitting on the wicker loveseat sipping lemonade, she decided Sara was falling to pieces, all regard to appearances cast away as though she didn't care anymore. She knew what lay behind it and sympathized with her friends, aware of what they were up against, and she ached for Jack, a proud man caring for his wife without complaint, and failing.

He arrived in minutes, winded after racing over to Sea Song. Sara greeted him with a radiant smile, forgetting Rose had called to invite him over.

"Jack, what are you doing here?" she asked, rising to give him a hug.

He crossed the patio floor with wide steps and pulled her toward him, a frantic expression in his eyes. "Are you having a nice visit?" he asked, pretending that finding Sara at Rose's house without him was normal.

They visited until their glasses were empty and it was time for Rose to prepare lunch. She watched her friends walk hand in hand down the drive, and leaned against the front door, filled with sadness.

Rose stretched out in her lounge chair and tried to return to her novel, to forget her pain and disappointment. She missed Sara, her near sister, her best friend. She missed their talks and their outings, the movies they shared, the meals they prepared side by side, the gardening, the card games, and their "missions" to the antique shops. She hadn't had a friend like Sara in a long time. She could never replace her, and didn't want to.

She sighed, shifted her position, and studied her back lawn cut in perfect rows. She and Stan hired professional landscapers to maintain their property. The task overwhelmed them. The house, too, wore them out, although neither admitted it to the other.

Rose was tired. Tired of housekeeping, tired of cooking, just plain tired. In addition, Stan had slowed down, his health deteriorating. Diabetes required him to stick to a strict diet and take shots of insulin two or three times a day. Years of smoking had damaged his lungs until he depended on inhalers and steroids to breathe. Added to this list of complications was his size; he was a bear. Once as muscular as a linebacker, he'd grown soft and doughy, with rolls of flesh hanging from his sides and a big beer belly leading his way. He tried to lose weight but lacked the discipline. He figured it was too late anyway; he was past eighty.

"Any new days I get are a blessing," he told Rose, determined to enjoy every minute of each one.

Both knew some adjustments were on the way—it was inevitable—but they had a plan for their old age. She'd made sure of it after years of caring for her mother. Rose refused to become a burden to her children. She would have done anything and more to see her own mother was comfortable, but she had to admit that providing her care had demanded great sacrifice. She and Stan had worked hard all of their lives, hoping to enjoy their retirement years with financial security and a family they'd raised with pride. Her mother's Alzheimer's had taken much of that.

Yet if she had to do it again, she wouldn't hesitate.

She reclined in her chaise lounge, the forgotten book in her lap as the sun warmed her bones. The summer heat comforted her and she yearned to store it inside, to suck it into her bones and save it for winter, when the wind blowing across the salt marsh made its way into her old house through its many cracks.

She tried to find her place in the novel, but the expression on Jack's face during their tour of Bayside Village haunted her and tears blurred her vision. Raising her fist to her mouth, she bit on her hand to stop the bitter flow of sadness, disappointment, and anger. How she hated this disease. It had taken so much from her: first her mother, then her supposed golden years, and now her best friend. It wasn't fair. Nothing in her life had prepared her for any of it.

She indulged in a few minutes of quiet weeping, but too practical to waste much time on self-pity, wiped away her tears with the hem of her T-shirt and picked up her book. The story she was reading promised to have a much happier ending than Jack and Sara's.

Chapter Twelve

David and Anne arrived at the hospital well past noon. They'd waited a half hour for David's tow truck and hit heavy traffic halfway down Route 3. The highway to the Cape was thick with vacationers, tourists, day-trippers, and commuters. David fumed while they idled at the base of the Sagamore Bridge, waiting for their turn to cross the Cape Cod Canal. He'd tried several times to reach Jack on his cell phone but failed, only adding to his frustration: he'd *told* his father to keep the phone handy.

They made their way to the fourth floor and headed for Sara's room. On the way, they ran into Sara's nurse, Julie.

Marianne Sciucco

"You're here for the Harmon's," she said when they walked past her. "They left about an hour ago."

David stopped in his tracks. "What do you mean, 'they left'? I told my father to wait here for me. We were planning to bring my mother to Bayside Village together. How could they leave?"

He'd called earlier that morning and talked with Allison, the case manager who had arranged Sara's discharge. He'd asked her to make sure his parents didn't leave the hospital without him and he thought she understood his concerns. Jack had mixed feelings about Sara's stay at Bayside Village, and David wanted to make sure everything fell neatly into place, no hassles. He hoped to ease them into the situation, to see they were both comfortable with the transition. He also wanted to oversee the financial arrangements; after all, this was business, too.

He'd done what he could by phone and fax to make the process smooth and easy, to spare his father any needless worry. Now something had gone awry, and Jack and Sara had left the hospital without him.

Not that he didn't trust Jack. They'd reached an understanding, albeit a silent one, that this was the best choice at this time. Although he trusted his father not to renege on their agreement, he worried about his reaction to the situation and was concerned about how he was

156

handling it. Jack insisted this was a temporary stay, but David believed once Sara adjusted to her new environment the best thing for both her and Jack would be to stay there permanently.

He was also uneasy about Sara's response to Bayside Village. She might put up a fuss in the beginning, but since she lost all track of time and needed to be reoriented over and over to the day and hour, to where she was, and to whom different people were, he figured she'd eventually forget about home. The situation was heartbreaking for all of them, but his mother had crossed some threshold in her illness that made her forget she had any sickness at all, and David considered that a blessing.

Still, another worry nagged at him. A few small dents in the rear quarter panel of his father's Lincoln had caught his attention. Jack claimed he didn't know what had happened, and assumed someone had bumped into his car in a parking lot and taken off. It had been months, and Jack hadn't had it repaired. This puzzled David. Jack always took impeccable care of his automobiles, and they were like new at trade-in time. No more than a minor fender bender marred his driving record. Any nick or dent in the car's finish upset him and he righted things immediately. David suspected *Jack* was bumping into things, although his father would never admit it. He tucked this new concern away for later, dreading the battle to take away Jack's driving privileges, especially now, with his mother living at Bayside Village and Jack's car his only means to see her at all.

"I don't understand. I thought I made it clear my parents were not to leave the hospital without me," David said. "Let me talk to Allison."

Julie went to the phone and paged the case manager.

David, furious, paced the corridor while they waited. Anne leaned against the wall and watched him.

Allison arrived at the nurses' station, Julie right behind her. "Mr. Harmon," she said. "Is there a problem?"

"Yes, Allison, we have a problem. You and I agreed I would accompany my parents to Bayside Village. You said you understood my concerns about my father taking my mother there on his own."

"Yes, I remember," answered the case manager. "I made the arrangements myself. Everything was in order. So, what happened?" she asked Julie.

"Dr. Fallon discharged her," the nurse explained. "I didn't know she couldn't leave with her husband. No one said anything to me about it."

"Did you read my discharge note?" Allison asked. She went to the desk, picked up Sara's medical record and pointed to the note she'd written that morning: "To be discharged to Bayside Village assisted living facility. Patient will leave with husband and son." She'd underlined the words "husband and son."

Julie read the note and shook her head. "I didn't see it," she said. "Mrs. Harmon always leaves with Mr. Harmon. I didn't even think about it." She turned to David. "I'm sorry. I didn't know we were supposed to wait for you."

David sighed. He shouldn't have relied on Jack to remember to wait for him. He should have called the hospital to tell the nurse of his delay and asked her to have his parents wait for him. Julie was right. Jack had always taken Sara out of the hospital before. It was only natural she'd leave with him today.

"Let's go to Bayside Village," he said to Anne. "They must be there by now."

They made it there in good time. The lunch rush was over and traffic had eased. As they cruised up the long drive toward the assisted living center, David commented on its beauty, noting the lush lawns, the well-kept buildings, and the people meandering across the grounds. He caught glimpses of the ocean from different points and smelled it in the breeze.

They entered the building and approached the front desk. The receptionist stopped typing and glanced up from her computer screen.

"I wonder if you can tell me if my parents have arrived," said David. "Jack and Sara

Harmon? They had an appointment for eleven o'clock. My mother is being admitted today."

The receptionist grabbed the phone and pounded in a number, all business. "Marlene, I have a gentleman out here at the desk inquiring about a Mr. and Mrs. Harmon. Could you please come out?" She listened and hung up. "Marlene will be out in a moment. She's the Admissions Director. Won't you please have a seat?" She turned back to her typing.

A moment later, a heavyset redhead greeted them.

"Mr. Harmon, I'm Marlene McHale, the Admissions Director." Her husky voice reminded David of a smoker. "It's so nice to meet you. We've spoken on the phone several times. How may I help you?" She drew closer, emanating acrid cigarette smoke.

He wrinkled his nose and stepped back. "Have my parents arrived?"

Marlene stared at him in confusion. "I have Mrs. Harmon scheduled to arrive by eleven. I spoke with Mr. Harmon yesterday. They haven't arrived. I was getting ready to call the hospital. Sometimes things happen over there and we get a little off schedule. I figured they were running late."

"They're more than two hours late. Why are you waiting to call?" David's voice rose. Anne tugged at his sleeve, a gesture they used to remind him to watch his temper. He took a deep breath and stretched his neck and shoulders.

Marlene hurried to defuse the situation. "I'm sorry, Mr. Harmon. I'll call the hospital right away and see what the problem is."

"They're not there. They left before eleven o'clock," David said before she picked up the phone.

"Well, perhaps they stopped somewhere on the way," Marlene suggested. "People often stop at home to pick up something they've forgotten. Or maybe they needed to shop for a few items on the admissions list: underwear, shoes, or toiletries."

David considered this while he chewed the nails on his left hand, a bad habit. "So, where are they?" he asked Anne. "Do you think he brought her home?" He knew Jack was reluctant to bring Sara to Bayside Village. Had he decided to forget about their plans and brought her home instead? If that was the case, he had another battle on his hands.

He reached for his cell phone and realized he'd left it in the car. "May I use your phone?" he asked Marlene. She nodded and escorted them back to her office. David called Blue Hydrangeas and listened to the phone ringing unanswered on the other end. After a dozen rings, he hung up. He dialed the number to his father's cell phone. A recording again advised him the caller was unavailable. "There's no

Marianne Sciucco

answer at the house," he said, "and his cell phone isn't turned on. I can't reach them."

"Maybe they're in the yard and can't hear the phone," Anne suggested.

"Maybe," he said, unconvinced. "Let's go to the house. It's worth a shot. They have to be home or on their way home. Where else would they go?"

Jack and Sara were homebodies out of necessity. She grew agitated and unmanageable in unfamiliar surroundings. Large crowds upset and confused her. Stores were overwhelming. In late afternoon, her confusion and agitation intensified, and Jack struggled to keep her calm. Dr. Fallon called it "sundowning syndrome," and said it was common with Alzheimer's. To compensate, they stayed home and Jack kept her in constant sight.

David and Anne drove to Blue Hydrangeas, hoping to find them having lunch on the deck or preparing to go to Bayside Village. David expected to see Jack's car when he pulled in, but found the driveway deserted. Dismayed, he parked in the circular drive.

They entered the house. Silence greeted them, punctuated by the steady ticking of the grandfather clock in the hall.

"Mom? Dad?" David called. He peeked into every downstairs room and headed into the kitchen. He tried the door leading to the deck and found it closed and locked. He went to the

162

window and scanned the back yard, seeing no one. He checked the garage —no Lincoln. Jack and Sara had not come home. They must have stopped somewhere. Once again, he tried to reach them on the cell phone and heard the recording that the caller was unavailable. He walked into the living room and plopped down on the couch.

"I don't know where they could be. Any ideas?" He shook his head and buried his face in his hands.

Anne joined him on the couch. "Maybe they went out to lunch." She sounded as worried as David. She adored Jack and Sara. Since her parents had passed on, her in-laws filled a painful void.

"Wouldn't they be back by now?" David checked his watch: half-past one. Jack planned to be at the hospital by ten. Julie said they left before eleven. That gave them more than two hours for lunch, and they wouldn't have ventured far, sticking to Falmouthport and somewhere close and familiar, like Cap'n Bill's.

"Call Rose Fantagucci," Anne suggested. "They might be there."

David dialed the number to Sea Song. The answering machine picked up his call. He left a brief message and hung up.

Where *were* they? None of it made any sense. His father hadn't given any indication he wouldn't follow through with their plan. Had he misunderstood Jack's intentions? Had he imagined Jack went along with this arrangement? He might have had no intention of moving Sara into Bayside Village and was simply humoring him. A silly thought, he decided. A lot of time and effort had gone into their arrangements. Jack must be in agreement.

Maybe they'd stopped at a store to pick up a few things for Sara. Maybe Jack needed to run a few errands, go to the post office, or pay a bill somewhere. Maybe he'd remembered to wait for David and returned to the hospital. He picked up the phone and dialed. The hospital operator put him through to Julie.

"It's David Harmon. My parents haven't returned to the hospital, have they?" He gripped the phone with a clenched fist and held his breath.

"No, Mr. Harmon, I'm afraid not. I haven't seen them since they left. Is something wrong?" Julie sounded frazzled. In the background, David could hear the hum and buzz of a busy medical unit.

"They never showed up at Bayside Village. We checked there first, and no one's seen or heard from them. We thought they might have gone back to the house, but they're not here, either. I'm running out of ideas. I don't know where they could be. My father didn't say anything about stopping anywhere on the way to Bayside Village?" David grasped at straws, desperate.

"No, I assumed they were heading straight there," she answered, sounding worried. "Hold on a second. Dr. Fallon just stepped off the elevator."

David heard Julie explain the situation to Dr. Fallon, who took the phone from her.

"Hi, David," the doctor said. "I don't know what's going on. I talked to your father last night and he said everything was okay. It was all set for your mother to go to Bayside Village. She seemed fine this morning when I examined her, best I've seen her in a long time."

"I'm worried," said David. He paced from the kitchen, to the dining room, to the living room, and back. "I have no idea where they are, and I'm concerned about my Dad's driving. I think he's had a few near misses."

"Well, maybe, but medically speaking your father's in good shape, all things considered. He told me last night his back pain was better and he'd stopped taking the muscle relaxants. It's okay for him to drive. I'm sure they're fine. They probably stopped for lunch, or needed to run a few errands. He should have taken her straight to Bayside Village, but maybe he didn't think they'd be this long. I'm sure they'll show up anytime now," Dr. Fallon tried to reassure him.

David called Bayside Village and spoke to Marlene, who had no news to report. He gave her the numbers to Blue Hydrangeas and his cell phone with instructions to call if his parents showed up. He promised to call her if he heard from them.

They agreed to speak to each other in an hour. He convinced himself everything was okay; they just needed to wait a little longer. If Jack and Sara failed to turn up by three o'clock, he planned to call the police.

Chapter Thirteen

Jack drove the Lincoln out of Bayside Village and turned back onto Route 28 toward Hyannis. He had no plan, no idea of where they were going, but he had to get away from that place. As beautiful as it seemed with its manicured lawns, blooming flowers, and cheerful, competent staff, it was still an institution, and he was not about to entrust Sara to its care.

Before their arrival at Bayside Village, he'd resigned himself to carry out this plan. He never intended to take her away before they made it inside, but the sight of the residents sitting on the porch—their dejection, their pitiful exteriors—shocked him. Sara didn't belong there. She was lovely and charming. Her clarity and good health this morning were encouraging. Their lunch at Cap'n Bill's had been wonderful, and the drive to Bayside Village full of pleasant conversation. He felt confident everyone was wrong, and he and Sara still had time. It was too soon for them to separate.

Why couldn't he continue to take care of her at home? He could get more help. The county sponsored a day care program for people with Alzheimer's. In the past, he'd rejected even that idea, but if he could have Sara at home with him most hours, he'd bring her there every day. Their staff would watch over her, keep her busy, and give him free time to take care of the house and meet his own needs. In the afternoon, he'd bring her home, and they would have dinner together and sleep in their own bed. Sara couldn't object to that. She was a sociable person. She might enjoy getting out on her own. He made a mental note to call about it first thing in the morning.

Jack merged into the traffic on Route 28 and concentrated on driving. At this hour, the height of the afternoon, the heavy traffic made him tense and nervous. These days driving around at any hour was getting more and more difficult. People went too fast, stopped short, and made quick turns right in front of him. He worried he wouldn't stop in time and cause an accident.

After several silent miles, he decided to turn off Route 28 and began making his way to

Route 6, the Mid-Cape highway. This route ran the entire length of the Cape, from Bourne to Provincetown. He eased the Lincoln onto the highway and headed east, cruising at fifty-eight miles per hour.

"Where are we going?" Sara finally asked. "Hyannis?"

"Too much traffic," he answered, still no destination in mind. All he knew was that he needed to drive, and drive fast. He thought for a moment, and an idea that had kept him up for far too many nights popped into his head.

"Let's go to the end of the earth," he declared. It was a long-standing joke with them ever since their first summer vacations on the Cape. "The end of the earth" meant Provincetown.

Geographically, Cape Cod was formed in the shape of an arm showing off its biceps, with Provincetown its fist. A seasonal town, its winter headcount of thirty-five hundred swelled to more than forty thousand in summer. It was an artists' colony and a favorite tourist and vacation destination. At the peak of Sara's art career, she and Jack had been regular visitors.

"Why are we going there?" Sara asked.

He shrugged. "No reason. It's just such a nice day. Maybe you can do some painting." He kept some art supplies and a few blank canvases in the trunk in case she felt the urge to paint during their daytrips. Their last excursion had been months ago, and although Jack tried to get her to capture something on canvas she hadn't been up for painting *en plein air*.

"We haven't been there in a long time," she said. "Do you remember the last time?"

Jack thought about it, but Sara beat him to the answer.

"Wasn't that the time we went to the show for that woman – oh, what was her name? Liz?"

Jack remembered and smiled. "Yeah, it was about five years ago. Her name was Liz. Elizabeth Crane." He thought, *Good girl, Sara. She remembered.*

"Well," she said, "it's a beautiful day. I can't think of a better place to go."

Jack nodded and set the car on cruise control. Provincetown was almost fifty miles away.

Less than an hour later, they went around the Orleans rotary and entered outer Cape Cod. Business was at full throttle on the farthest end of the Cape in July. Cars with license plates from all over clogged the roads. Jack plodded along behind them, mindful of the speed limit, ready to brake at any moment. They soon entered the town of Wellfleet, home to one of the last drive-in theaters in New England. Sara laughed and clapped her hands when she saw it.

"It's still there," she said, a look of wonder on her face. "Oh, Jack, remember when we used to take the kids to the movies? They'd take over the back of the old beach wagon and we'd camp out in front of the screen, letting them snack on all the popcorn and grape soda they wanted." She traveled back in time, reliving happy memories, animated, her face alive.

Jack lived for these moments. Most of the time she was poker-faced, and it frightened him for he'd always been able to read her mind by the expressions on her face. As her Alzheimer's progressed she so often wore a mask, and he had no idea what went on behind that mask, if anything. Did she dream? Did she think happy thoughts? If so, she kept them to herself and left him wondering. Right now, she seemed spirited and exuberant and his spirits lifted. She might not remember what they ate for lunch, but she remembered tucking the kids into the back of the old Jeep Wagoneer with pillows and quilts and letting them pig out on Grape Crush and Cracker Jack.

After passing the old drive-in, they moved through Wellfleet and into Truro. It was here that Sara had first achieved recognition as an artist. The small seaside town encompassed fourteen miles of the outer Cape and was famous for its breathtaking beaches, one of America's oldest golf courses, and a historic lighthouse known as Cape Cod Light. Its year-round population of two thousand stretched to more than twenty thousand during the summer months.

Truro had changed in the years since their last visit. New building and development were everywhere. Pricey Cape Codders with water views dotted the landscape. Jack gaped at the size and extravagance of these structures, doubting he could have ever afforded such a home, despite his robust IRA.

They approached the exit for Truro Center. Sara pointed at the sign marking the turnoff and said, "Oh, there's the road to downtown Truro. Why don't we stop?"

Jack resisted, afraid of where it might lead them. Their times in Truro were filled with memories, most of them happy ones, but on this day, he wanted to avoid a trip down Memory Lane, to prevent Sara from remembering why they'd closed the Corn Hill house for the last time and never returned. "Let's keep going," he said. "We'll be in Provincetown in a few minutes."

Sara's eyes flashed with determination and she dug in her heels. She could be so like a child when she wanted something and he stood in the way. "No, Jack, let's go into Truro. We haven't been there in so long."

Jack knew when he couldn't win and he didn't want to upset their day. An argument would spoil everything. With a great sigh, he prepared to make the turn. They'd pass through town and get right back on the highway. Surely, that couldn't hurt.

Downtown Truro was small: a post office, fish market, liquor store, and a general store. He parked the car by the general store and they watched the foot traffic. SUV's crowded the parking lots, stuffed with kids, boogie boards, and beach gear. Beachgoers entered and exited the stores, picking up snacks and supplies. The memory of doing the same tasks infused Jack with nostalgia. He'd always said a person could spend a whole day on the beach, dawn until dark, if he had the essentials: food, family, and friends. That was the lure of the beach, and it had once incited Jack as strongly as it did any of these young fathers setting off to enjoy the afternoon with their families.

A few minutes later he asked, "Do you want something? A cold drink? Something to eat?"

"I'll take a lemonade, please," Sara said, and he went into the store. Cold drinks in hand, they headed out of Truro.

Jack, anxious to get on their way, followed the road through town and got back on Route 6. Not a mile later, Sara noticed the sign that led to the turnoff to Corn Hill.

"Corn Hill," she read. "Remember, Jack? We stayed in that cute cottage on the bluff, the one with the deck on the roof. I could see the beach and watch the kids play while I worked." She turned around in her seat to look back as they passed the turn. "Stop," she ordered. "Go back. Let's go see the old house."

Jack couldn't help but let out an impatient groan. "Why?" he asked. "We haven't been there in more than twenty years. No point in going now." He continued to drive.

Sara remained undeterred. "I want to see the old house. It'll just take a minute. I don't see what all the fuss is about."

"I don't see what all the fuss is about, either." Jack pulled over and slammed on the brakes, causing them to pitch forward. A car passed on the left with a blast of its horn. "Now, let it be. We haven't been there in years. I don't want to spoil the day by visiting the past."

"I want to see the house," Sara insisted. "Why can't we just drive by?"

Jack closed his eyes and counted to ten. Powerless, he sagged against the seat. She asked for so little these days.

He checked for traffic in his rear view mirror and turned the car around. As they slowly cruised down Corn Hill Road toward the bay, they searched for the old house. They'd used this road for years but he felt like he'd never been there before. He remembered it was at the end of the road, set back a bit on the left, but a development of new homes now consumed the bluff where it had once stood. Jack drove to the end of the road and parked the car.

"It's not here," he said, studying the area. "It used to be right there." He pointed to where a new house, still under construction, rose from the sand with decks and balconies on all sides and walls made of windows. It was spectacular. Similar homes surrounded it, each one boasting an expansive view of the bay. He failed to remember this spot at all.

They emerged from the car. This place seemed unfamiliar, yet he felt a deep connection to it. He listened to the sound of the beach, to the waves tumbling against the shore. The scent of beach roses floated on the breeze. The hot sun caressed the top of his head. In the distance, he heard the sound of children at play.

He took Sara by the hand and they started along a footpath that led to the top of the bluff. In just moments, they stood overlooking Cape Cod Bay. Beach blankets lay corner to corner on the crowded beach. For a few moments, they watched children build sandcastles, bodysurfers jump into the pounding waves, and sunbathers soak in the sun. Across the bay, they saw the Provincetown Monument towering over the old fishing village.

Jack's heart rate accelerated. He had hoped to live out the rest of his life without ever visiting this place again. It was a beautiful spot, yet held such ugly memories. Twenty-seven years ago, their daughter, Lisa, had drowned here, right off this beach. He'd vowed never to go back, and they hadn't, until now. He leaned against Sara to steady himself, gazing out over the bluff as bitter memories consumed him.

It was a Friday night, the start of a week's vacation, and Jack planned to spend the last week in August with his family at their summer rental. Medical conferences in other states had prevented him from visiting the last two weekends, and he couldn't wait to see Sara and the children. The following Saturday they'd pack up and go home.

He'd approached the house and pulled up slowly, hoping he was in the wrong place. Police cars and emergency service vehicles filled the driveway. Sara sat on the porch, surrounded by police officers, neighbors, and friends, her face red and tear-streaked, her eyes swollen from sobbing. David sat next to her, looking about the same.

She was far too hysterical to explain what had happened. The police officer in charge took him aside and broke the news. There had been a terrible sailing accident and Lisa had drowned.

Sara and David filled in the rest. Although Jack had given strict orders that Lisa and David were not to sail the catamaran alone, she'd gone out on the bay by herself. She'd asked David to take her, but he had said no, too much wind, and promised they'd go later if the wind died down. She'd spun on her heel, raced out of his room, and slammed the door behind her. She launched the boat, paddled out into the harbor, and raised the sail. It was her first summer as a sailor and her skills were weak. She lost control of the boat when an unexpected squall kicked up and overwhelmed her.

It was late afternoon, the light at its best, and Sara stood on her rooftop deck at work on a watercolor of a neighboring cottage, its weathered shingles and bright pink trim an inspiration. Beach roses surrounded the house. Laundry hung on the line and fluttered in the breeze. She'd admired the scene all week and was ready to paint it. She saw the catamaran enter the water and smiled. They'd bought it that summer, given the kids lessons, and felt comfortable with David at the helm. She had no idea Lisa maneuvered the boat on her own, while David lounged in his bedroom, also unaware of his sister's solo sail. She went back to her work, paying little attention to the catamaran, other than to notice how it drifted peacefully across the water.

Moments later, the wind kicked up, knocking her canvas to the floor. Paints and brushes scattered all over. She stooped to pick up her tubes of paint and caught sight of the boat's sail flapping unsecured. The catamaran bounced uncontrolled on the waves. The sea looked rough, much rougher than she wanted it with her children adrift. She saw the boat keel to one side and noticed someone struggling with the mast. Odd, she saw only one person onboard. She picked up the binoculars she kept with her art supplies and looked again, confident she'd see David. She shrieked when she saw Lisa operating the boat alone. She dropped the binoculars, bounded down the stairs, and raced through the house to get to the beach.

"David," she screamed. "Where are you? Lisa's in trouble."

The nineteen-year-old lay sprawled on his bed, headphones blaring Pink Floyd. Sara burst into his room and cried, "Lisa's out in the boat. She can't handle it."

They ran out the door and headed for the beach. A crowd had formed to watch the catamaran founder. Its useless sail flapped in the wind, and Lisa's pitiful cries for help echoed back to shore. The lifeguard's shift had ended. David grabbed a small rowboat lying on the sand and headed into the surf.

"I'll go with you," said another young man and they shoved off.

"Hold on, Lisa," David called, plunging the oars into the water. He kept his eyes on the catamaran, watching it toss and turn in the waves like a piece of driftwood. Lisa had lost all control. The waves were heavier, higher, and more powerful the further he rowed out. The harder he pushed forward, the farther away he seemed from the floundering catamaran.

The boys struggled with the small boat and quickly became exhausted. The waves pushed against them, preventing them from making much progress. David lost sight of his sister each time a wave came between them. A huge one careened against the boat and they almost capsized. They regained control, and David searched the pounding sea for Lisa. He saw the catamaran upended, his sister nowhere in sight. He passed the oars to his companion, cupped his hands around his mouth, and shouted her name, hoping she'd surface on the other side of the cat.

Minutes passed, seeming like hours, and at last they approached the catamaran. David jumped into the water and grabbed onto the cat, searching for his sister, calling her name. His deep voice echoed over the beach, where his mother watched the sea threaten to rob her of both of her children.

The police arrived and launched their own rescue boat. David stayed near where he last saw Lisa, guiding the search effort. Close to an hour passed before they found her with a gash on the side of her head. The boat had struck her when it capsized, rendering her unconscious. There was no way she could have saved herself.

David returned to shore in the rescue boat alongside his sister. Sara threw herself at the boat when it landed, her cries piercing the beautiful summer day. David clambered out and held his mother. The crowd hung back, parents clinging to their children, muttering, "What a shame."

Sara and David watched the rescuers lift Lisa from the boat and lay her on the sand. They attempted CPR but it was too late, and after a few minutes, they gave up. A policeman brought the catamaran back to shore and laid it to rest in the sand. Another officer escorted Sara and David back to the house. A crowd had gathered, concerned neighbors offering comfort and support. Jack was due in an hour. They sat vigil and waited for him.

How could it have happened? Sara and David blamed themselves for not paying enough attention to Lisa. They blamed her for being headstrong and for not following the rules. It was irrelevant. No matter who was to blame, she was gone.

The event devastated Jack. He'd worked all of his life to provide for his family, to give them the best life had to offer. He marveled at the absurdity: his daughter lost while she enjoyed the best he could give her. *If only,* he thought, again and again, throughout all of these years, these decades. If only I had been there. I could have taken her out in the boat. I could have done something, anything, and she would be here today. If only....

There were hundreds, thousands, of memories, of recriminations. He blamed himself for his daughter's death. That it was a freak accident, a matter of poor judgment on her part, of poor timing, of bad luck, didn't enter his thoughts. He'd bought the boat. He'd encouraged the children to learn how to sail. He had only himself to blame.

Now, here he stood, in the spot where he'd experienced his most profound loss.

Sara stood firmly in the sand, supporting him. The salty breeze whipped through her hair. Her face was free of worry. "Isn't it lovely, Jack?" she asked as she gazed out over Corn Hill Beach.

Jack could barely form words. He took deep breaths, struggling to compose himself, bracing for Sara to remember what had happened here, and to fall apart. "Yes," he muttered at last, his throat tight, his voice strained. He brushed away the tears that stung his eyes.

"Jack, you're crying," she said, wiping away his tears. Her cheeks and eyes were dry. She linked her arm with his, helping him to maintain his footing.

He latched on to her, letting the tears fall. They stared out toward the sea, listening to the rush of the tide, the squawk of seagulls, and the cries of children playing on the beach. It was as if time had not passed, and they were still the parents of teenagers with the best of their lives ahead of them. He couldn't believe all of that was over.

When Jack regained his composure, he gestured toward the car and they walked back holding hands. He settled into the driver's seat and sat paralyzed behind the wheel for a few minutes pondering what had happened.

Why had he brought them here? Was this encounter a coincidence, or did their spur of the moment journey into the past have a deeper purpose? Had he meant to expose Sara to reliving this horrible event, to trick her memory into remembering the worst day of her life? And for what? He'd been so careful to keep her from remembering Lisa's death. He'd thought she wasn't strong enough to confront the agony of that day.

Yet, he had been wrong. His fears had been unfounded. Sara had no memory of what had happened here, and if this brush with reality failed to remind her that they once had a daughter they'd adored, a beautiful young girl taken from them in an instant, she would never remember Lisa.

Maybe he'd brought them here to ease his own pain, to vanquish his own wrenching memories. He couldn't forget, and what did that get him? Sleepless nights. Heartache. Guilt. Forgetting would be welcome, a blessing. Instead, he bore the burden of remembering for both of them.

Chapter Fourteen

It was blistering hot on the back nine of the Falmouthport Golf Club, no breeze, and Derek sweated like a marathoner halfway through the race. He'd forgotten how brutal it was to caddy eighteen holes in the July heat, but he could not turn down the opportunity to caddy a second round.

He wiped a bandana across his brow and took a long sip from the bottle of water hanging from his belt. The water was warm, but wet. He dumped the rest of it over his head, picked up Mr. Henshaw's bag, and followed him and the rest of his foursome across the green. They reached the final hole just after two o'clock.

When his grandfather had called with news of a summer job at his golf club, Derek was thrilled. Caddying for Jack's golf cronies meant good money. Many of them tipped him extra simply because he was Jack's grandson. He also picked up some pointers on his own game. He'd joined the junior golf league and played on his days off.

The only drawback was that most of the men he caddied for were old, retired businessmen, and *boring*. Their talk of the stock market, the weather, and where they went and what they ate for dinner the night before nearly killed him. At least this shift ended soon, and he'd take a short break before he changed into his red trunks and headed for the pool, on duty as lifeguard until six o'clock.

Lifeguard duty was a party compared to caddying. Free of tedious old men, he kept an eye on pretty girls in skimpy bikinis, their bronze skin glowing with suntan lotion as they roasted themselves on the pool deck. He enjoyed watching them, and they knew he was watching, keeping vigil from high up in his lifeguard chair. He had yet to rescue anyone, and doubted he ever would, but the younger kids kept him busy with their horsing around.

Lifeguarding was a nice way to chill out after lugging golf bags around all morning for a bunch of long-winded old men, and it beat last year's job of bussing dinner tables. He sat on his butt until closing with hot babes fawning, and sometimes even fighting, over him.

He followed Mr. Henshaw, tuning out the recitation of yet another business deal that had made a million bucks for one of the old geezers. Mr. Tucker was talking. He was a fat guy with a bad toupee sliding back and forth across his sweaty head. Derek feared it would fall off, obliging him to pick it up. Tucker was married to a woman Derek and his friends referred to as "The Babe," a well-preserved forty-something trophy wife the other caddies claimed was ready to jam with anyone other than her husband. She'd given Derek a wink and licked her lips when her husband lumbered off with the rest of his foursome. Derek passed. He preferred girls closer to his own age: less baggage. But he smiled back, unwilling to offend her and perhaps lose her husband's hefty tips.

Although preoccupied, Derek performed his job flawlessly. No one would guess his mind was a million miles away, besieged with worries about his grandparents.

He knew about his grandmother's condition, but what concerned him most was his grandfather. Without Sara at home, Jack moped around the house, wandering from room to room searching for something, anything, to do. This lonely, listless Jack seemed so unlike the grandfather he knew so well. When Sara was home, Jack was a whirl of motion, dragging her around with him, keeping her occupied, anticipating her every need. Just watching him exhausted Derek. The amount of attention his grandmother required amazed him. *High maintenance,* he'd determined after a few days at their house.

Derek hadn't spent any considerable time there in months, and when he showed up to start his summer with them it appalled him to see how much Sara had changed. When he arrived, she didn't even know who he was, which shouldn't have surprised him.

Last Thanksgiving had been a disaster. His family had gone to Blue Hydrangeas and his parents had helped Jack lay out the usual holiday feast. After dinner, the guys crashed in the family room, sprawled across sofas and armchairs, snoozing, watching a football game, or simply digesting while they waited for dessert. Sara and Anne washed the dishes and then joined them. Sara entered the room first and stopped halfway, alarmed at the sight of the four men spread all over. She saw Derek lying on the couch and pointed at him.

"Why is he here?"

Jack popped out of his recliner, his post-feast rest disturbed. "That's Derek, our grandson," he explained. "He's supposed to be here."

Sara grew agitated and confronted Derek, standing before him with her hands on her hips, a wild look in her eyes.

"Who are you? What are you doing in my house?" she shouted, gesturing toward the door. "You get out. Go on. You don't belong here."

The room grew silent except for the TV blaring the third quarter. Everyone grew uneasy. David and Anne explained that Derek was their son, her grandson. Jesse crammed himself deep into a corner of the couch and threw a blanket over his head. Derek approached his grandmother plaintively, trying to reason with her.

"It's me, Grandma, Derek," he explained, but Sara was beyond reasoning.

After convincing her that Derek was not an intruder but someone who belonged with them, Jack escorted her upstairs and settled her down. He tucked her into bed and returned to the family room to apologize to David, Anne, and the boys. Good food, wine, and brandy had flowed generously that afternoon, and the adults attributed Sara's increased confusion to overindulgence.

"Grandma's not herself," Anne explained. "Her forgetfulness should be expected. It's not that she doesn't love you. She can't help it. It's the Alzheimer's."

Still, the incident had shaken the boys. Derek, seventeen, was devastated, and silently wept all the way home.

At his arrival this summer, he again wanted to cry when his grandmother opened the door for him and stared at him as though she had never seen him before, a polite smile on her face.

"May I help you?" she asked as though he was a guest, and Derek suddenly felt like one.

"Grandma, it's me, Derek," he said, frightened she'd slam the door in his face. He braced for her reaction, but smiled with relief when Jack appeared beside her and welcomed him with a big hug.

"Look who's here, honey. It's Derek, David's youngest boy. He's here to spend some time with us this summer. Isn't that nice?"

Sara recovered and gave her grandson a perfunctory hug. It hardly resembled the comforting embrace he'd treasured as a child. He shook off his disappointment— perhaps she'd warm up to him over time.

He fell into their routine and helped Jack around the house, doing light housekeeping, washing the car, and watering the garden. He enjoyed his summer. The money was great, pretty girls were everywhere, and he had somewhere fun to hang out every night.

Yet, the plight of his grandparents disturbed him. His grandmother was another woman, so different, a stranger. He'd spent every birthday, holiday, and summer vacation with Jack and Sara. Their lives meshed so perfectly. He saw all of that changing, and it filled him with apprehension.

His father had called that morning to talk to him about his grandmother's move to Bayside

Village. He'd never been to such a place, had never seen one, and shuddered at the idea of visiting one. Weren't these places full of old, sick people who reeked of urine, couldn't take care of themselves, and had no one else to care for them? How could his father and Jack even think of leaving Sara in such a place? Blue Hydrangeas was her home. Why couldn't she stay there? Why couldn't Jack hire some nurses to live with them? They couldn't cost more than what Bayside Village would cost.

He thought about the house. The Blue Hydrangeas he'd known was about to vanish. With Sara gone, the house was not the same. It was, and always had been, her house. She was its life, heart, and soul. A visit to Blue Hydrangeas was a retreat, an escape from the pressures and problems of the real world. It evoked a mystical quality, a feeling that time stood still, of hours devoted to simple pleasures. Even at his young age, he knew this, and he knew he wasn't alone in his feelings. He'd worked at the house when it was full of people. He'd helped his grandparents accommodate their guests, served breakfast, washed dishes, and did whatever else they asked. He witnessed the responses of their visitors. People fell in love with the inn, and all because of Sara. She had a way about her that made them feel well cared for.

Derek was a practical young man, but he wondered and worried about everything, warranted or not. Before he left home for the summer, he'd raised his concerns to his brother, Jesse. The two lay stretched out in a pair of black leather recliners in front of the TV, watching the Red Sox take a beating from the Yankees. Like their mother, they were born Red Sox fans, and it set them up for heated debates with their father and grandparents who were staunch Yankee fans. It made for an interesting season.

"It'll be weird at Grandma's this summer," he said during a commercial break.

"Boring is more like it," Jesse replied, dipping into a bowl of salted cashews, exhausted from a long day at his construction job. He hated the work and looked forward to returning to his studies, although he was transferring to the school where his parents worked and was sure to run into them or their dopey intellectual friends every day.

"I'm talking about Grandma. I never know what she's going to do or say," Derek explained, rolling over to face his brother. The boys were not alike at all. Derek resembled their father: fair and freckled, pale auburn hair, hazel eyes, and the lean body of a swimmer, muscled in all the right spots. Jesse favored Anne: blond, olive-toned, and blue eyed, with an athleticism that had made him the captain of his high school's football team.

"She's crazy," he said, and popped another handful of cashews into his mouth. He sat up straight, better to catch a triple play in the making. He cursed at the third baseman and relaxed.

"Don't say that about Grandma," Derek bellowed, the game forgotten. "She's sick; she has a brain disease. She can't help it."

"She's crazy," Jesse repeated, his attention riveted to the TV.

"She's not crazy. I'm just saying it's not going to be the same at the house with her the way she is. Grandpa tries, but he doesn't know how to do things the way she did them. It's not the same."

"Nothing is the same. That's life. They're old. It happens," Jesse said. He was the less compassionate of the two, almost twenty and full of himself.

"Grandpa seems sad," Derek continued. "He follows her around, makes sure she doesn't get hurt, and makes sure she takes a bath and eats. He can't leave her alone for a minute, not even to take a crap. He leaves the door open when he goes into the bathroom. I walked in on him once."

"He's crazy, too," Jesse answered, focusing on the game. The Yankees scored and he swore at the TV.

"They're not crazy, Jesse. She's sick and he's doing his best to take care of her. Why can't you see that?"

Jesse turned off the TV and stared at his brother. Careful to choose his words, he said,

"I know she's sick. Don't you think it bothers me? I love Grandma. But, there's nothing we can do about this. She won't get better, Derek. You have to face it. If Grandpa doesn't get help to take care of her, he won't last, either. It sucks, but that's how it is. I'm with Dad: I think she needs to go live in some old folks home, give Grandpa a break before she kills him."

"Grandma will never leave Blue Hydrangeas. Grandpa will never let that happen."

"That house is too big for the two of them, Derek. There are eight bedrooms. It's a lot of work for Grandpa, even if he does have a housekeeper. They need to scale down. They should sell the old place and buy a condo."

Derek was horrified. The idea had never occurred to him. "Now *you're* crazy," he said. "Grandpa will never sell that house."

"Don't be too surprised if he does," Jesse replied. "That old folk's home will cost a fortune."

"Grandpa has tons of money," Derek said, not one hundred percent sure of Jack's financial status.

"Maybe. Maybe not. We'll be lucky if there's anything left for us." Jesse turned on the TV to catch the last inning. Red Sox were down, six to two.

"I hate you! How can you even think like that?" Derek cried. He jumped from his chair and bolted out of the room.

"It's something to think about," Jesse shouted after him. "And so is this: Alzheimer's may be hereditary, which means you and I can get it."

Derek slammed the door behind him, not wanting to hear anymore, not willing to allow his brother to see his tears. Everyone thought they were being smart, reasonable, and responsible about their decisions regarding Sara. Didn't anyone care what she wanted?

As he cleaned up after caddying and prepared for his pool duty, he put the conversation with Jesse behind him. He had a sick feeling in his stomach. Something was wrong. He checked the time. A few minutes remained before he had to relieve the lifeguard. He made a quick call to Jack's cell phone, and ended the call when it went to voicemail. A sense of foreboding gnawed at him, but it was time to get back to work. He headed for the pool area, and at first sight of a sixteen-year-old in a cheetah-print bikini forgot all about Jack and Sara.

Marianne Sciucco

Chapter Fifteen

Jack and Sara arrived in Provincetown just after two o'clock. The town was alive with activity, and Jack decided not to waste time driving around in circles in search of free parking. He drove to MacMillan Wharf and paid for a spot in the municipal lot.

Hand in hand, they strolled through the town center, blending in with a diverse crowd of people: young families pushing baby carriages, senior citizens, straight couples, same sex couples, the tattooed, the pierced, and the nearly naked. Provincetown was a haven for those who found its generous acceptance a necessary port in a sometimes bitter and intolerant world. July was its peak season, the week after Independence Day one of its busiest.

Thousands of people mobbed the streets, lining up to fork over their money to the seasonal vendors along the way.

Jack and Sara walked down Commercial Street, peering into art galleries and critiquing the work. Some of the art they liked. Some was too abstract or modern for their tastes. Jack decided to buy a new piece for the house to remember this special trip. Sara's good spirits and clarity of mind on this day had given him hope, hope for a new beginning, and the belief that the plans to take her away from him had been premature, and they might continue as they had before, at least for a while.

They whittled away the afternoon with window-shopping and crowd watching. Jack's stomach rumbled and he checked his watch: four fifteen. They hadn't eaten in hours.

"How about a cup of chowder from The Lobster Pot?" he suggested.

"Yes, and coffee, too," Sara answered.

He took her by the elbow and escorted her across Commercial Street. A line of people waited to get into the Lobster Pot. Outside, people sat on a low brick wall talking on cell phones, sipping cold drinks, and resting their weary feet. Jack led Sara to an open seat on the wall.

"Sit here and wait for me," he instructed. "I'll go in and get us the chowder and coffee. I'll only be a few minutes. You sit right here and don't go anywhere, okay?"

"Sure," she said, making herself comfortable on the brick wall. "I'll people-watch. I'll let you know if I see anyone interesting."

Jack went into the restaurant, peeking back over his shoulder to keep an eye on her. Several people were ahead of him in line at the takeout counter, many of them sucking down Wellfleet Oysters and littlenecks at the raw bar, clogging the take-out area, and getting in Jack's way.

As he sidled up to the counter, he looked back over his shoulder frequently to check on his wife. She remained perched on the brick wall. He wasn't worried about her wandering off. Although the afternoon was waning, she'd been clearheaded and cooperative all day. Besides, he'd only be gone a minute.

Ten minutes passed before he gave his order to the man behind the counter. Another ten passed before he made for the door, supper in hand.

In this brief time, the crowd queuing up for The Lobster Pot had grown and blocked his view of outside. The restaurant grew noisy, a steady din rising as the crowd thickened. A roll of thunder stopped all talk for a moment. Heads craned toward the windows. Clouds had set in, obscuring the sun. A wicked wind kicked up, blowing litter across Commercial Street.

Jack pushed through the throng of chattering tourists. "Excuse me," he said, clutching his package. He squeezed through the crowd, pushing against bodies and stepping on toes until he made it outside. He labored to catch his breath before turning toward the brick wall, expecting to see Sara watching the street action, but she wasn't there. A young woman wearing a bikini bathing suit top and bicycle shorts had taken her place. Jack turned in a circle, searching the crowd to see if she'd moved to another spot. She was nowhere in sight.

He ventured on to Commercial Street, sidestepping people as they dashed into shops and stores in search of shelter from the impending downpour. They pushed and shoved against him, hindering his view. His heart skipped a beat each time he saw a white-haired woman, but none were Sara.

With a sinking heart and a desperate sense of foreboding, he realized he'd lost her. She'd walked away from him into this monstrous mass of strangers and he had no idea where to start searching for her. He studied his surroundings, noting all of the buildings she could have wandered into.

The crowd rushed past him, bumped into him, distracted him with its noise. Heavy thunder boomed and fat raindrops fell from the sky. He felt a deep pain in the center of his chest. His skin turned moist and clammy. He fumbled for the little vial of pills in his pocket and slipped one of the nitroglycerin tablets under his tongue.

With the bag containing their supper tucked under his arm, he waded through the crowd, hoping to find a police officer. Two stood on the opposite corner. He hurried over to them and explained the situation. The policemen eyeballed each other.

"How long has she been missing?" asked the tall one.

"I don't know," Jack answered, thinking hard. "I went into the Lobster Pot a few minutes ago to get us something to eat and left her there, sitting on the brick wall out front. I told her to stay there, to wait for me, and I watched her from inside the restaurant. It got crowded and I couldn't see her anymore, and when I came out, she was gone. And now it's raining." Jack wiped his brow, now damp with sweat and rain.

"She's probably in one of the stores," the older policeman said. "She probably got tired of waiting and decided to browse a bit. You know how women are."

"You don't understand," said Jack. "My wife is not well. She has Alzheimer's." The hated words slipped easily from his tongue and elicited the desired effect. The policemen snapped to attention. They moved Jack out of the rain to a sheltered spot under an awning. One cop pulled out his radio to notify the dispatch officer they had a missing person with altered mental status. The other cop took out his notebook and began firing questions at Jack.

"What's your wife's name? What does she look like? What is she wearing? Does she know where she is? How well does she walk?"

Jack answered as best as he could, each question increasing his anxiety. He'd always feared losing Sara and dragging the police into it. Now, on a hot July day, in the late afternoon, in a downpour, two policemen in the middle of a boisterous Provincetown crowd were quizzing him about her disappearance. Again, he felt the pain in his chest and reached for the little pills. The questioning policeman noticed.

"Sir, are you all right?" he asked. Jack wiped his brow. He felt weak and needed to sit down. He looked for a seat, a bench, anything. The policeman grabbed his elbow. Taking the package from Jack, he said to his partner, "Hey, Lou, I think we need an ambulance for this guy." He led Jack to a small sidewalk café, waved the hostess away, and seated him in an empty chair under an umbrella. The other cop followed, barking orders into his radio for an ambulance.

Jack couldn't catch his breath. The air was thick and moist and he sucked at it in tiny, gasping breaths. A crowd had gathered to watch.

A police car and an ambulance arrived in minutes. Two additional police officers consulted with the others, and then worked their way through the crowd in search of Sara.

The paramedics loaded Jack onto a stretcher and into the ambulance. One placed an oxygen mask over his face. The other checked his vital signs and hooked him up to EKG leads.

"Sir, what's your name?" she asked.

He gasped out his name.

"Mr. Harmon, is there someone we should call?"

Jack mumbled the number to David's cell phone.

The paramedic gave the information to her partner who went to the cab of the ambulance to make the call. A few minutes later, he returned and reported David was on his way.

Jack nodded and mouthed, "Thank you." Raindrops beat against the roof of the ambulance.

"Mr. Harmon, given your symptoms and the fact you're carrying nitroglycerin tablets, you're most likely suffering from angina, but it's possible you're having a heart attack. You need a doctor. We have to take you to the hospital immediately," explained the woman paramedic.

Jack shook his head. "No," he whispered. "No heart attack. It's angina. Because of the stress." His words came in quick, choppy succession. "I won't go anywhere until we find my wife. She's not well, you know. It's my fault. I shouldn't have brought her here."

"Sir, I understand your concern for your wife, but you need immediate medical attention," the paramedic said.

Jack pulled the oxygen mask off his face and sat up. "Let me out of here. I'm not going anywhere without Sara."

The paramedic placed her hand on Jack's arm. "Please, Mr. Harmon, you are making things worse." She pointed to the machine tracing his heart rhythm on its screen. "Please sit back. We'll try to stabilize you here in the truck, but you need to be in a hospital," She handed him the oxygen mask.

Jack grimly nodded and put it on, but stood his ground. "You're not taking me anywhere until we find her," he repeated.

The paramedics glanced at each other. The woman shrugged. "I'll call the medical director," she said. "We'll see what he says."

Chapter Sixteen

When three o'clock came and went with no word from Jack and Sara, David checked with Marlene at Bayside Village and Julie at the hospital but neither had seen nor heard anything. He dialed Jack's cell phone every five minutes and each time got the same message: "Caller unavailable." His worry escalated with each unanswered phone call. It wasn't like Jack to remain unreachable for so long.

"None of it makes any sense," he said as he paced between the living room and dining room. "My father is a responsible man. He'd never do anything to put my mother in harm's way, especially now."

Which led to his other fear—something had happened to Jack, leaving Sara to deal with it on her own. He might have had a heart attack.

They could be laying in a ditch somewhere, the car run off the road, one or both of them injured. A dozen different scenarios flashed through his mind. He didn't see how his mother could handle any emergency.

He considered going out to find them, leaving Anne at the house in case they called or came back, but he didn't know where to start and the effort seemed futile. Instead, he called the police.

A squad car arrived in minutes. Two officers entered the house and followed David into the living room. Anne remained on the couch where she and David had waited out the last hour, tense and anxious.

"How long have they been missing?" asked Castaldo, the lead officer. He'd arrived on the scene with his partner, a wisp of a girl who looked barely out of her teens.

"They were last seen before eleven this morning." David reviewed the day's events. "I've been calling him all afternoon, but his cell phone's not turned on. I haven't spoken with him in about five hours."

"Is there anywhere they may have gone?" Castaldo asked. "Maybe they stopped somewhere along the way and lost track of time."

"I doubt it," David said. "They don't go out too often. It's hard for Dad to take my mother anywhere. When she's having a good day he might take her out to eat or for a walk. The
204

people at the hospital said that today was a good day, but lunch or a walk wouldn't take this long. They should have turned up somewhere by now." He continued to pace the length of the living room, a nervous habit.

"Is it possible they ran into some friends, or stopped to visit someone on the way?" Castaldo pressed on.

David considered it. Jack and Sara had many friends, although in recent years they rarely socialized. They might have stopped somewhere to visit, or bumped into someone on their way and decided to take a coffee break.

"It's unlikely," he said, "but I'll call a few people and see if anyone's seen them."

"That's a good start," answered Castaldo. "We'll call the dispatcher and have him put out an alert. I need the make, model, and year of the car, a license plate number, that type of information. We'll call the hospitals and police departments in the area to see if they might have had an accident or are in one of the emergency rooms. Also, can I get a recent picture of them? We'll make copies and get them to the rest of the on-duty officers."

The younger officer took notes. "I'll call the dispatcher," she told Castaldo. He nodded and followed David to get the picture.

Castaldo and his young rookie left the house with a photograph in hand, a nice shot of Jack and Sara taken at the golf club's Memorial Day barbecue.

David found his parents' address book tucked into a desk drawer and started dialing on the house phone. He called a number of people, many of whom were not home, and left messages for them on their answering machines. Those who answered his call said they hadn't seen Sara and Jack recently and sounded surprised to hear from him. The more calls he made, the more discouraged he became. It was after four o'clock. After twelve calls, he was still in the "B's." He could spend hours on the phone and get nowhere. He gave a great sigh and turned to Anne.

"I don't know," he said. "It's not like them to be gone for long. Something must have happened. This isn't good."

Anne went to him and took his hand. She hugged him and he buried his face in her hair. A phone call from a paramedic in Provincetown interrupted their embrace.

David and Anne jumped into her Volvo wagon and sped away from Blue Hydrangeas. The ride from Falmouthport to Provincetown took about ninety minutes. David hit the Mid-Cape highway and set the cruise control at seventy-five miles per hour.

Anne rode next to him and tried to ease his fears. "They'll find her, they have to," she said. "How far can she go, anyway? It's a small town. Someone is bound to notice her and report her to the authorities."

"Anne, we don't know what state of mind she's in. What if she's having one of those sundown episodes? She's probably confused, lost in a mob of strangers, and angry and agitated because of it. She could strike out at someone, causing more confusion and commotion. Anything can happen," David said.

"And my dad," he continued. "He could be having a heart attack. Whatever possessed him to take a ride to Provincetown? They haven't been to the outer Cape in years and he took her there today? Why didn't he wait for us at the hospital like I told him to? None of this would have happened if he had just cooled his heels and waited for me." His face tightened with worry, his knuckles rigid over the steering wheel. Over the last few months, his concerns for his parents had been escalating, but that wasn't all that kept him up at night. The last year had been full of turmoil and he didn't know if he could handle any more.

It all started in the fall when Anne found a lump in her right breast. Her mother and an aunt had died of breast cancer, and her doctor ordered a full workup that lasted for several nerve-wracking days. They kept their anguish from Jack and the boys, reluctant to cause worry about something that might turn out to be nothing. Still, they worried. They walked on eggshells throughout the ordeal, and waited through sleepless nights and tension-filled days for the final word. When it came, and it was good, they heaved a shared sigh of relief.

Only weeks later, David received a call from the dean of students at Jesse's school, a small private college in Connecticut. Jesse was in the hospital. His roommates had found him unconscious and unarousable after a heavy night of drinking. The doctor said it was acute alcohol poisoning; his blood alcohol level had been more than twice the legal limit. He might not make it through the night. David and Anne rushed to his side. After a long night, Jesse awoke, stable but with a horrendous hangover.

Once he was capable of managing conversation, David and Anne questioned him about what had happened. A freshman preparing for a career in journalism, Jesse had only been on campus a few weeks before joining a fraternity known for its heavy drinking. Heady with his newfound freedom one hundred miles away from the watchful eyes of his parents, he became a binge drinker.

Frightened for their son's future, Anne and David yanked Jesse out of school and took him home. He went to work full-time for a friend of David's who ran a multimillion-dollar construction project in downtown Boston. They figured that ten to twelve hours a day of hard, physical labor would cure him. He came home at night worn out, ate dinner, watched TV, crawled into bed, and rose at five the next day to go back to work. Little time remained for a social life, and most of his friends were away at school.

Jesse continued his backbreaking labor throughout the summer. In the fall, he'd get back to school, but this time he'd live at home and commute to the university where his parents worked.

Anne's cancer scare and Jesse's near death by alcohol poisoning only added to the tension caused by Jack and Sara's issues. Their situation had been brewing for years, and Jack seemed to have things under control, but lately their problems were intensifying with staggering urgency.

While Sara's condition had degenerated slowly, Jack's health was rapidly deteriorating. He was failing, and witnessing his decline pained David. Last winter he'd seemed full of life and energy, but two days ago, he seemed like a wizened old man, beaten and taciturn, consumed by Sara's illness and the relentless caregiving he felt driven to provide at any cost.

David was glad Dr. Fallon had called on the evening of Jack and Sara's latest calamity to let him know of Jack's rising difficulties in caring for his mother. He'd been waiting for that call, suspecting the situation would come to a head at any time, and sooner than he thought.

David understood that he and Anne belonged to "the sandwich generation," baby boomers caught between bringing up children and caring for aging parents while they approached their own middle age. He'd read about it but was ill prepared for this phase of his life. Suddenly, David had to make tough, heartbreaking decisions.

They approached the Orleans rotary, less than thirty miles from Provincetown. While David had silently brooded about his recent problems, storm clouds had gathered over Cape Cod, and rain was now pelting the car.

"You've got to be kidding," he said. "My mother is lost, wandering around Provincetown in the rain?" He pushed down on the accelerator and upped the cruise control to eighty-five miles per hour.

Chapter Seventeen

Downtown Provincetown was the scene of an intense search effort. At least a dozen police officers and volunteers combed the streets, searching for Sara in every store, every restaurant. A tense thirty minutes had passed when a young officer named Esther Mendoza made her way up Commercial Street, away from the hustle and bustle of the town center, and entered a small art gallery. It was crowded with people who sipped wine and sampled cheese and crackers. The event was an exhibit for a local artist that had earned much press and publicity.

Mendoza made her way into the gallery and the crowd parted to allow her through. A cop in full uniform was a strange sight in this place. A woman stood behind an elegant oak desk and gestured for Mendoza to come over. The officer approached and the woman hung up the phone.

"I was about to call the police," she said. "There's a strange lady here. I think she's lost, you know, confused." She pointed to an elderly woman with white hair in a disheveled French braid. The woman paced back and forth in front of a painting, mumbling to herself.

"How long has she been here?" asked Mendoza.

"Not long, about twenty minutes. She came in and started walking around. I offered her a glass of wine and she walked right by me. She headed for that painting of the blue flowers and just stood there," said the woman. "By the way, I'm Cynthia Armstrong. It's my gallery. This is an exhibit for Marcia Cleary. It's called, 'The Outer Cape in Bloom.'" She handed Mendoza a program.

Mendoza folded the program and stuffed it in her back pocket. She surveyed the gallery and admired the watercolors of landscapes bursting with bountiful wildflowers, interspersed with paintings of well-planned gardens that were resplendent in sunlight. They were beautiful in their simplicity and clarity.

She stared at the old woman who stood in front of a large painting of blue hydrangeas arranged in a small wicker basket. The flowers were the color of the sky at noon on a clear day. The basket rested on a windowsill. Filmy white curtains framed the window and fluttered in the breeze. The window looked out on a harbor, a sailboat floating in the background. The scene was reminiscent of many summer cottages on the Cape at the height of the summer season.

The old woman was studying the painting with great interest and talking to herself. She reached out to run her fingers along the picture frame. Mendoza approached her with care.

"I know this painting," the woman was saying. "I've seen it, but I don't know where. Oh, I'm so mixed up."

Mendoza tapped her on the shoulder. "Sara?" she asked. The old woman startled. "Are you Sara Harmon?"

The old woman stared at her with eyes the same summer blue as the hydrangeas. "Who are you?" she asked.

"I'm Officer Esther Mendoza of the Provincetown Police Department. What's your name?"

"Why are you here? Shouldn't you be in Provincetown?" Sara asked, her voice rising above the din of the crowd. She took a step away from Mendoza. The gallery grew quiet. The party had stopped and people were watching them.

"Ma'am, you're in an art gallery in Provincetown. Do you know how you got here?"

Mendoza spoke gently, reluctant to agitate the woman.

Sara hugged herself tight and eyed the crowd. "Who are all these people?" she asked.

"It's an art exhibit. They're here to see the paintings. Is that why you came here? For the paintings?" Mendoza tried to make conversation with the woman who she assumed was the missing person.

Sara glanced around her surroundings. She recognized no one, but she knew the painting. She'd seen it earlier, when she and Jack had passed the gallery on their stroll down Commercial Street.

She'd grown restless waiting for him to get their dinner, abandoned her spot on the brick wall, and wandered away. She'd walked about five blocks before stopping in front of the gallery, where she again noticed the painting visible from the huge picture window in front. It called to her, and she went inside to get a closer look. The gallery was jammed with people talking and laughing. Music played in the background, underscored by the sound of glasses tinkling against one another. The high-pitched ringing of the phone grated on her nerves. The noise rose to a crescendo, making her afraid and confused, alone in the midst of a crowd. She couldn't understand what anyone said. She didn't know where she was or how she'd arrived there.

However, the painting captivated her, and she stood before it, desperate to remember something, anything about it.

"I like this painting," she told Mendoza.

"Do you like art?" Mendoza asked.

Sara nodded.

"Are you an artist?"

"I don't know," Sara answered with a frown.

"Are you Sara Harmon?"

"How do you know my name?"

"I've been looking for you. Jack asked me to find you. He's worried about you."

"You know Jack?" Sara asked, eyebrows arched, a glimmer of comprehension in her eyes. "Where is he?"

"He's waiting for you, down the street where you left him. Would you like me to take you there?" Mendoza reached out her hand, but Sara shook it away.

"No," she said. "I'm staying here." She stepped away from Mendoza.

The officer sighed and watched her walk away. She asked the gallery owner for a chair and brought it to Sara. She pulled her cell phone out of her pocket and called her supervisor to report she'd found the missing person safe and unhurt. She gave him their location and stood behind Sara, waiting for help to arrive.

Jack lay on a stretcher in the back of the ambulance. The police notified him at once that Sara was safe.

"Thank God," he said, smiling. "When can I see her?" His condition had stabilized.

"Soon," answered the woman paramedic. She adjusted the oxygen tubing dangling from his neck. "I heard Sara found her way to an art exhibit and doesn't want to leave. There's an officer staying with her until your son arrives."

"Sounds like Sara." He grinned. "She'd spend all day in an art gallery. She's an artist you know."

"That explains everything. She's sitting in front of a painting of some blue hydrangeas in a basket, and she won't budge. She says it seems familiar to her."

"Of course," said Jack. "She was known for her paintings of blue hydrangeas. She has a magnificent garden of them back at home. They're her favorite flowers, you know."

"I'd like to see some of her work. I'm an artist, too, a potter. I built a little studio in my garage."

"Her work hangs all over the Cape," Jack boasted, "even here, in Provincetown. Sara donated a bunch of paintings to the town. There's one in Town Hall, one in the library, and a few up at the high school."

"I'll have to check them out," the paramedic said.

Jack's chest pain had resolved and he hadn't required any more nitroglycerin tablets since the second. His breath came effortlessly and his skin was warm and dry. Still, he needed to see a doctor and they had lost enough time.

"Your son will be here soon, Mr. Harmon," the paramedic said, "and I can assure you your wife is safe. Please let me take you to the hospital. Your family can meet you there."

Jack nodded. Although he wanted to see that Sara was safe with his own eyes, he understood he had to attend to his own needs. Plus, he didn't want her to see him strapped down in the ambulance with the oxygen mask and intravenous; it would only upset her. David was on his way. He'd take care of her.

"Let's go," he said.

The paramedics secured the ambulance and they were on their way to the hospital in Hyannis.

Marianne Sciucco

Chapter Eighteen

Sara remained at the gallery under the watchful eye of Officer Mendoza and stared at the painting, riveted. She didn't know why, but it filled her with peace and tranquility.

A young woman with long, dark hair approached her. A collection of silver bracelets glittered on one arm. A pair of broken-in Birkenstocks covered her feet, the toenails painted red.

"Excuse me, Ma'am," she said to Sara. "I'm the artist. I noticed how much you like this painting."

Sara smiled up at her and took the slender hand she offered. She held it close and examined it. She drew the woman's hand up to her face and inhaled deeply. The faint scent of oil paint emanated from her fingers.

"I love that smell," she said, setting the hand free.

"Do you paint?" the artist asked.

Sara stared past her and didn't answer. A commotion at the front of the gallery had caught her attention. A man and woman were walking toward her. "I know that man," she said and rose from her chair to greet him. "You're here," she said, patting David's arm.

David threw his arms around her and held her close. He examined her with a practiced eye, convincing himself she was okay.

"Look at this," she said, pointing at the painting. "Isn't it lovely?"

David looked at the painting and caught his breath. If he hadn't known better, he'd have sworn his mother had painted it. Sara's work was superior, but this was good. It looked just like the one that hung in his foyer. She'd painted it that last summer in Corn Hill, the summer when Lisa died. One morning, before anyone woke up, she set her easel by the kitchen sink and painted the view from the kitchen window. He remembered waking up that morning to find her deep in concentration, lost in her creativity as she covered the canvas with her crisp, colorful strokes.

"Yeah, Mom, it's beautiful. Do you want it?" It would brighten Sara's new home at Bayside Village.

She nodded. "Yes, I do. I want it very much."

"We'll take it," David told the artist.

They headed back to Hyannis. With the help of the police department, they'd located Jack's car and Anne followed David and Sara.

They drove in silence, Sara dozing, her head resting against the window. David was still uneasy about the day's events and worried about his father. He'd called the hospital and learned the Emergency Room doctor was running some tests. Dr. Fallon was on his way. They couldn't tell him much more.

Traffic was light until they reached Hyannis. Summer visitors in search of dinner and some nightlife flooded the streets. He marveled at the crowd. He hadn't visited Hyannis on a summer evening in years. The town vibrated with energy.

They managed to wend their way to the hospital. Inside, they raced to the Emergency Room and a nurse led them to Jack. They found him lying on a stretcher in a curtained cubicle. He seemed pale and tired. Dr. Fallon was examining him, his heavy stethoscope held against his chest. Sara rushed to Jack's side.

"Where have you been?" she asked. She leaned in to give him a kiss, pushing aside the oxygen tubing wrapped around his face. "What's all this? Are you all right?"

"Jack's fine," the doctor said. "We checked him out. Just a spell of angina. What about you, Sara? How are you?"

"I'm fine," she answered, "but I want to go home."

"It's been a long day," said David. "Mom, why don't you go home with Anne and I'll stay here with Dad? We'll come home as soon as Dr. Fallon says we can leave." David, alarmed by the doctor's grave expression, suspected he had spared Sara the frightful details of Jack's condition. They needed to talk, and it would be best for all if Sara left the noisy Emergency Room.

"Yeah, Mom, come home with me," said Anne. "We'll sit out on the deck and have some dinner while we wait. I'm sure Jack and David won't be too late."

"Good idea," Dr. Fallon said. "No need to hang around here. I can't let all of you stay in the ER with him, anyway. You might as well go home."

"Are you sure it's all right?" Sara asked Jack. He nodded and she leaned over to kiss him goodbye.

"I'll see you later, honey," he said, returning her kiss.

The women left. Silence filled the cubicle while each man debated what to say next. Jack's thin voice broke the silence.

"All right, I know you're mad at me. I did something stupid. I didn't mean for all of this to happen. I didn't mean any harm, especially to Sara. I guess I got carried away."

"What's happening, Doctor?" David asked. He stared at Jack with a sinking heart. His father's pale, thin face poked out from under the skimpy, white hospital sheet. His long, bony limbs formed peaks and valleys under the covers. He'd aged these last few days. His face now sagged into wrinkles. The twinkle in his eyes had gone out. He looked like a lost, little old man. David caught a view of himself in a mirror on the opposite wall and his own appearance shocked him. He looked like he'd gained at least five years himself.

"Your father's had another heart attack," Dr. Fallon explained. "Not a bad one, but I'm afraid we have to send him up to Boston for another bypass. His heart's not good, David. There's been a lot of damage over the years, and the vessels we operated on before have started to collapse again."

David nodded as the doctor spoke. Everything seemed to be happening at once: his mother's worsening dementia, the need to move her to a facility where she'd have twenty-four hour care, and now this. He didn't know how to respond. He was angry with Jack for not bringing Sara to Bayside Village and for putting her in harm's way. He was sad they could no longer care for her in her own home. He was frightened Jack's heart was failing.

"Tell us what happened, Dad," he said. "Whatever possessed you to take Mom to Provincetown? What were you thinking?"

Jack grimaced. "I couldn't bear to leave her in that place, not even for a week or a day. I made a mess of things," he said, his voice trembling before he broke down in tears.

David reached for the privacy curtain and pulled it closed. "That's why I wanted you to wait for me. I wanted to go with you when you brought Mom to Bayside Village. Why didn't you wait for me?"

"They packed Sara up and said we could go, so we went. I forgot all about you until we got to the place, and then it was too late. I shut off the phone because I knew you'd try to reach me and I didn't want to talk to you."

"Dad, this day has been coming for a long time. You tried your hardest, I know you did, but it's time to let go."

"I can't let go," cried Jack. "I don't want to live without her. And don't try to tell me I can visit her every day and call her on the phone. I don't want to visit her or call her. I want to wake up in the morning and have her beside me, and I want to kiss her goodnight in our own bed. These are our final years and we have to spend them apart?"

David sighed and dragged his fingers through his hair. "Dad, I'm sorry, but we've talked this over dozens of time. We have to make the best of the situation and do what's right for all of us, especially Mom. I can't let you kill yourself trying to control the situation. The most we can do is see that Mom's taken care of and to stay involved with her for as long as possible."

"He's right, Jack," added Dr. Fallon. "You gave a good fight. Remember what I told you back in the beginning? Alzheimer's disease is bigger than both of you. It's time to let go."

"The hardest part is sending her away from home," Jack said. "Blue Hydrangeas was her dream, and I spent my life making it real for her. I can't bear to live there without her. I'll see her wherever I go, in every room, outside, everywhere. How will I do it, David? How will I go home without her? I'll rattle around, lost in that big empty house all alone."

David heard the despair in his father's voice. "Maybe you don't have to," he answered thoughtfully. "Dr. Fallon," he continued, "aren't there apartments at Bayside Village where couples can live together?"

Dr. Fallon was way ahead of David. "I know those apartments. Your parents may be perfect candidates. First, we need to take care of your father's heart. In the meantime, what will we do about your mother?"

"Anne and I will stay at the house with her until Dad's ready to come home. We'll move them to Bayside Village together."

Jack looked beyond the two men planning the next phase of his life, and focused on the opposite wall, resigned. "Whatever you think is best," he said.

"We'll see how you make out in Boston, and when you're ready, we'll do this together,"

David said. "I'll talk to the people at Bayside Village and make the arrangements."

"Are you sure? I don't want you to sacrifice—" Jack began, but David cut him off.

"We'll do it, Dad. Don't worry. We're here for you." It was the least he could do for his parents. Staying with Sara for a few weeks was no burden. Margie and Mrs. Wright would help. Derek was around, and perhaps Jesse could visit for a few days. Sara might enjoy the company. David began mapping out his plans for caring for his mother.

Chapter Nineteen

After work, Derek joined some friends for a game of volleyball on the beach before going home to an empty house. He noticed immediately that Jack's car was not in the driveway, which was unusual because Jack was always there when he got home from work. His grandfather would ask about his day, sit with him while he ate a quick dinner, and ask if he needed any money before he went out for the night. Tonight, the house was strangely quiet and looked untouched since that morning. The day's mail lay on the floor by the front door. The refrigerator offered nothing for dinner. The message light on the answering machine blinked incessantly. *Where was Jack?* Derek wondered. He should be home by now.

Derek listened to the phone messages and his worry grew into alarm when he heard several people calling to see if Jack and Sara were all right. Derek speed-dialed the number for his father's cell phone and David picked up on the first ring.

"Hey, Derek, everything's okay," he said before Derek could say a word. "I'm at the hospital with Grandpa. We had an incident today, but Grandpa and Grandma are okay. Your mother will explain everything. She and Grandma are on their way home and should arrive any minute. Stick around tonight. We need to talk."

Derek heard the front door open and hung up the phone.

His mother looked beat as she ushered Sara into the house. His grandmother seemed tired, but not unlike she usually did at this time of day.

"Mom," he said as they moved into the kitchen. "What's going on? I talked to Dad. Is Grandpa all right?"

Anne held up a finger, gesturing him to wait a minute. She escorted Sara to the bathroom, switched on the light, and left her there with the door ajar. She went back to the kitchen and joined her son at the table.

"Grandpa didn't admit Grandma to Bayside Village like he was supposed to," she explained. "He took her to Provincetown, she wandered away from him, and he lost her. The police had to help him find her. She's all right, but I think Grandpa may have had a heart attack."

"Are you kidding?" Derek couldn't believe that steady, reliable Jack had done something so crazy.

"I wish," his mother replied. She started at the beginning, briefing him on all that had happened that day. As she told the story, it grew more and more unbelievable. How could Jack have taken such a risk? What was he thinking?

Sara emerged from the bathroom and took her seat at the table. Anne motioned to Derek to change the subject and then put on a pot of coffee. A long night lay ahead.

They heard a knock at the door and Anne found Rose Fantagucci on the doorstep.

"I was at the beach all afternoon and just heard David's message. Is everything all right?" Rose asked

Anne let her in, fixed them each a cup of coffee, and then brought her to the family room where she told her the story.

"That's not like Jack," Rose exclaimed. "He never takes Sara far from home these days, and they never go anywhere that's crowded. Something's not right. I saw him just this morning. He didn't say anything about not going to Bayside Village. I know he's miserable about this, but I never thought he'd do something dangerous."

"It does seem rather desperate," Anne agreed. She rifled through a stack of photographs strewn across the coffee table. They were pictures of David and his sister, photographs composed and preserved for eternity by their mother. Jack must have been looking at them, she surmised; perhaps that's why he snapped. "I can't imagine anything more horrible than this. I'm watching it happen and I still don't believe it. It's as if she's gone, but there she is. I see her, touch her, and hear her, but she's not there, is she?"

Rose shook her head, tears in her eyes. "No, and it gets worse. We mourn our loss now, and we'll mourn again when she leaves this earth. Turning my mother's care over to strangers, even trained strangers, was the hardest thing I ever had to do. I can't imagine doing it with Stan."

The women sat in silence, lost in their memories, humbled by a disease that had taken so much and was still taking, never sated.

Derek interrupted them. "Grandma's hungry. Are you making dinner or should I call for something?"

Anne downed the last of her coffee and got up. "I'll throw something together," she said. "She probably can't wait for a delivery."

It didn't take long for David and Anne to discover that caring for Sara was more than a full-time job. They were exhausted in less than two days.

She wandered the house at all hours in search of Jack. "Where is he?" she asked, repeatedly.

"He's at the hospital, Mom."

"Why is he at the hospital? He's not sick."

"He's having an operation."

"What operation? Will he be all right? Why didn't anyone tell me?"

They assured her they'd told her all about it and that he'd be fine, but their answers only increased her anxiety. After the umpteenth time, they switched their tactics, and told her he was out shopping or playing golf and would be back soon. She accepted their new explanations without question.

They lost sleep from the first night. Anne had helped Sara into bed around ten and Derek turned in a while later. David and Anne stayed up past midnight to discuss the situation. David was worn out, worried about his father, and had difficulty falling asleep. He drifted into a light slumber, thrashing about the queen-sized bed, bumping into Anne and disturbing her rest. In the middle of the night, he heard noises from downstairs. Moving like an intruder, he followed them to the kitchen. All the lights were on, the doors to all the cabinets were open, and Sara stood at the counter arranging a stack of mixing bowls. Canisters of flour and sugar, jars of spices, and the electric mixer were sprawled across the countertop.

"What's going on, Mom?"

She hadn't heard his approach and jumped at the sound of his voice. "Oh, it's you. You scared me. I'm making breakfast, that's what's going on."

"It's four o'clock in the morning. Go to bed. Make breakfast later."

"No, I always make my muffins now. I have a lot of work to do. We have guests and they'll be hungry."

"Ma, we have no guests. You, Anne, Derek, and I are the only ones here. You can go back to bed," he said, but she wouldn't listen. She rattled on, growing more agitated. He gave up, started the coffee, sat at the kitchen table, and watched her bake.

Anne stayed with her in the morning while he went back to bed. After breakfast, she dispensed Sara's medication, following Jack's instructions to the letter. She laid the pills on the table with a glass of orange juice.

"I know what you're doing," Sara said, and pushed the pills away, across the table, back toward Anne.

"I'm giving you your medicine," Anne explained. She was tired; she needed coffee and a shower, and didn't want any arguments. She pushed the pills back across the table.

"That's not my medicine." Sara pushed the pills away again.

Anne was confused. Had she given her the wrong medicine? She double-checked the pill bottles, matched the pills up against them, and verified she was correct.

"No, this is right. You take these pills at breakfast, and you take the pink one again after supper. The big ones are your vitamins and calcium."

"I know what you're doing," Sara repeated.

The tone in her voice chilled Anne. "What am I doing?" she asked.

"You're trying to poison me."

"I'm not trying to poison you," Anne exclaimed, shocked by the accusation. "It's your medicine. You take it every day. It's nothing new, Sara."

"It's poison," she said, jumping out of her chair and running out of the kitchen. You're poisoning me!"

Anne raced after her, yelling, "I'm not poisoning you."

David, roused by the commotion, appeared at the top of the stairs disheveled and disoriented. "What's going on?"

"You're poisoning me. It's all poison," his mother was shouting. "I won't take it. You can't make me. Police! Police!" She went into the bathroom and slammed the door.

David and Anne stared at each other.

"I was giving her the medicine," she explained.

"I guess we'll have to try again later," David

said, and went back to bed.

Most afternoons, Sara settled down. She napped for a few hours after lunch on the days they didn't drive into Boston to see Jack. David and Anne took turns running errands while she slept. They didn't leave her alone, and she didn't go anywhere without them.

For the most part, Sara was pleasant and easy to be around. She didn't ask for much, but when she was confused or agitated she turned into someone else, someone they didn't know, and they hadn't developed the necessary skills to manage her. David marveled that his father had held on for so long. He would have caved in long before this. He wondered if he'd be as strong if the same thing happened to him and Anne. He couldn't imagine his wife ever having dementia, but it had happened to his mother, which proved anything was possible.

In spite of having to provide for Sara's unending care, David and Anne enjoyed their stay at Blue Hydrangeas. While Sara was napping, they relaxed in her garden, camped out on chaise lounges under the shade of a majestic oak tree. David read the books he'd longed to read all winter, and Anne worked on the revision of a novel she'd written now under contract with a literary agent in New York. It made for pleasant afternoons. At night, they sampled each of the guestrooms. Their favorite was The Dunes. Its soothing and evocative colors reminded them of the beach at Race

Point Light, the barren seashore at the tip of the outer Cape.

It was when they stayed in Sara's favorite room, The Garden Room, that they made a harrowing discovery. Anne went to store some personal items in the drawer of an antique bedside table and let out a cry.

"Oh, David, you've got to see this."

He emerged from the shower, peeked into the drawer, and saw it contained a stockpile of medication, a colorful collection of capsules and tablets. He scooped them out, laid them on the bed, and started counting. He soon gave up. He and his wife locked eyes.

"The 'poison'," Anne said.

"My mother," he whispered. "How long do you think this was going on?"

Anne shook her head.

"Months, maybe," he continued. "She must have snuck in here and hidden them. She hated taking medicine. She rarely took an aspirin. Wait till I tell my father."

"Tell Dad?" Anne asked. "I don't think that's a good idea. He's having a hard enough time with losing this battle as it is. Do you think he needs to know? What difference will it make? He'll feel worse she fooled him and he never caught on."

David thought for a moment and nodded, agreeing with her. "You're right." He gathered the medicine into both hands. "I'll get rid of these pills and we'll never mention it."

For most of their marriage, they'd climbed into bed at night each with a book of their own, and read for a few minutes before turning out the lights to go to sleep. With all that had happened, they changed their routine, and held hands in the dark, talking until they dozed off. They wasted no time together. They'd learned every second was precious. Free of distractions, they made love more often and woke fulfilled and satisfied, a joyful way to start the day.

Two weeks passed. Emily and Ed came to visit for a few days, enabling David and Anne to spend a few days at the beach and head into town for dinner and a movie.

Another week passed before Jack's doctors released him from the hospital. Back at Blue Hydrangeas, he supervised David, Anne, and Derek from his recliner while they packed what he and Sara needed at Bayside Village. They made a smooth move into the new apartment. David and Anne stayed on until early August, making sure his parents settled into their new home before heading back to Boston to enjoy the waning weeks of summer.

Chapter Twenty

Autumn descended on Cape Cod with clear skies, a temperate climate, and softer shades of New England's brilliant fall foliage. Marsh grasses turned a muted yellow, scarlet and gold covered the maples and oaks, and the blue hydrangeas faded and dried. The Cape's inimitable light turned golden. The children had all gone back to school, the tourists were starting to call it a season, and the residents prepared to hunker down for the winter.

Jack's eightieth birthday fell on a Sunday in October, and David and Anne planned a private celebration. They reserved their special table in the dining room of the Falmouthport Golf Club. The party was small in consideration of Sara's fragile condition. Emily and Ed, Rose and Stan Fantagucci, and Derek and Jesse shared this special day with them.

Sara was radiant. Anne had taken her shopping and they bought new dresses. Sara's was the color of sapphires and brought out the blue of her eyes. The pearl choker Jack gave her on their twenty-fifth wedding anniversary adorned her graceful neck, and the diamond earrings she'd received somewhere along the way to their golden anniversary sparkled at her ears. Her snowy hair curled about her face and flowed over her shoulders. She seemed happy, aware something special was going on.

Sara's adjustment to life at Bayside Village had gone better than any of them had expected. At first, she was confused and disoriented, wandering from room to room, asking nonstop when they were going home.

"Why are we staying here, Jack? I want to go home."

"We're staying here, Sara," he said. "I need the help. Try to like it, okay? For me?" he pleaded.

Jack's words failed to comfort her. "When can we go home?" she asked, and he cringed each time. How could he tell her they weren't going back to Blue Hydrangeas?

He'd considered bringing her there for a visit, to check on things, maybe sit in the garden for a while, or walk over to Sea Song to call on Rose and Stan, but the Bayside Village staff discouraged him, explaining it would only confuse her and make the situation unmanageable. He agreed, and visited the house on his own making sure everything was okay. However, the visits depressed him, and he soon stopped going.

Day by day, Sara fell into her new routine, comforted by the dependable flow of time. Meals came on schedule, her personal attendant arrived when expected, and the staff arranged her activities and carried them out as planned. She grew comfortable in her new environment and soon stopped asking when they were going home.

Jack took great care to see that their apartment was full of comfortable and familiar objects. They'd moved in some of their bedroom and living room furniture, Sara's art supplies, and all of her photo albums. They packed up the essentials for the small kitchen and left behind the china and silver. Jack brought along his golf clubs, his computer, the television, the DVD player and VCR, and their movie collection. He kept his expensive stereo system and most of the music. They abandoned their gardens, their luxuries, and her studio. Rose and Stan adopted the cats.

They reestablished their special routines in their new residence, took their walks on the grounds of Bayside Village, and had their coffee and ice cream out on the private little patio outside of their kitchen. It wasn't Blue Hydrangeas, but it was home.

Jack had few responsibilities in their small apartment. A nurse or an attendant was a buzz away if he needed one. Sara's personal attendant came every morning to help her bathe and dress and made sure she took her medicine. She did light housework and checked with Jack to make sure there wasn't anything else they needed before she left. Someone else came in for the laundry.

He owned his time and spent it as he wished. He had several hours each day to play golf, read the newspaper, or visit with some of the new friends he'd made. No longer bearing the burden of caring for Sara on his own, he gained a few pounds and walked with a spring in his step.

On the Friday before his birthday party, Jack paid a visit to his lawyer. He had one more thing to take care of.

When David, Anne, and the boys arrived for the party, he took his son aside and closed the door to the bedroom behind them. He held a plain white envelope in his hand. He turned it over in his palms as he spoke to David.

"First of all," he said, clearing his throat, "I want you to know your mother and I are proud of you and we love you more than anything. We couldn't wish for a better son, or a better family. We love all of you, and want what's best for you. I appreciate all you and Anne have done for us these last few months. I know it wasn't easy, and I know I made things difficult for you."

David interrupted, but Jack held up his hand. "No," he continued, "I have to say this. I'm giving you something that has always been yours." He handed him the envelope.

"Here is the deed to Blue Hydrangeas. The house is yours, along with everything in it. You've taken care of it these last months, and you, Anne, and the boys were to have it someday, anyway. I'm giving it to you now so I can see you enjoy it. We never talked about it, but your mother and I wanted you and Anne to run it again as a bed and breakfast. We enjoyed our years as innkeepers. It was a shame we had to stop, but you know what happened. I'll understand if you don't want to get into the business. It's your house. It's your decision. But I would like your word that you'll keep the house for the boys as my legacy to them."

"Dad," David said, accepting the envelope. "I don't know what to say. Anne and I always dreamed of running Blue Hydrangeas the way you and Mom did. Are you sure about this?"

Jack nodded. "You were right, David. I have to let go of many things, and this is one of them. What am I going to do with such a big house? Even if your mother passes on before I do, I don't want to live there without her. I'm much happier here with the two of us in our little place. I don't have to worry about the plumbing, the yard work, shoveling the walkways, anything. I'm done. That part of my life is over."

David nodded, threw his arm across Jack's shoulders, and drew him close. "Thanks, Dad," he said, hugging him.

Jack patted him on the back. "Let's get back to the party," he said.

They left the bedroom and joined the others.

Anne and the boys were sitting with Sara, catching up on what was going on in their lives. Jesse, done with construction work, was back in school. Derek had started his first year at college and was adjusting to life away from home with little trouble. Sara listened to their talk, smiling and nodding at the appropriate moments. No one knew how much of the conversation she followed, but she seemed relaxed and content and that was all that mattered.

At the restaurant, a beautiful table was set with fresh-cut roses and champagne at every setting. David made the toast. He raised his glass and waited for the others to join in.

"To my Dad, a great father and a good man," he said. "May we continue to be blessed with his presence and love for many more years."

"To Jack." Everyone tipped his or her glass in his direction. Jack sat at the head of the table embarrassed but beaming, pleased with the attention.

"And to my parents," David continued, "who have been blessed with more than fifty years of marriage and have weathered many storms. They are an example to all of us of commitment and dedication. May their love continue to grow and nurture all who are fortunate to receive it." He raised his glass to Jack and Sara and everyone else followed suit. The women grew teary. The men cleared their throats.

Jack turned to Sara and gazed into her eyes. "To us," he said.

And, for a split second, the expressionless mask that usually hung over her face, the one that deprived him of any glimpse into her mind or soul, disappeared. She gazed back at him in a moment of perfect clarity, and said, "To us."

The End

Marianne Sciucco

Book Club Discussion Questions

1. Jack and Sara are members of "The Greatest Generation." In what ways does this impact their relationship? How does this affect Jack's commitment to care for Sara?

2. Jack and Sara are financially well off. In what ways would this story be different if they were not?

3. There are a number of voices in this story: Jack, David, Derek, Rose, Sara. How do these voices enhance the story? Are these additional voices unnecessary? Distracting?

4. The seasons play a large part in the telling of the story. In which scenes do we see winter? Spring? Summer? Fall? How do these seasons impact the story?

5. The blue hydrangeas have a major impact on the lives of Jack and Sara. Name all the ways these flowers have added to the richness of their lives.

6. Sara seems to have forgotten the loss of her daughter. Is this a blessing?

7. Jack's pride and stubbornness often conflict with his ability to care for his wife. How does this affect the rest of the family? Do the others who care for Sara have a right to be part of the decision making regarding her care?

8. The story is set on Cape Cod. Could this story be told anywhere else?

Author's Note

Writing this book was a labor of love, started more than ten years ago when I decided I would write a story and it turned into a short novel. So many people were helpful and supportive throughout this long and arduous process, made more difficult due to painful repetitive strain injuries that derailed my nursing career and threatened to take away the one thing I yearned to do all of my life: write. I would have given up long ago, and Jack and Sara's story would have remained stored on my computer's hard drive, without the support of family and friends.

At the top of the list is my mother, Marge Clairmont, who has always believed in me and whose prayers move mountains; my husband, Lou, who put up with my evenings holed away in my office and fell asleep in spite of the clickety-clack of the keyboard across the hall; and my daughter, Allison, who understood my need to write and gave me the freedom to do so. My youngest brother, Kenn Kasica, another writer, provided me with inspiration and encouragement and wouldn't let me give up. Jeffrey Kasica, my middle brother, kept me in his prayers and by his own example of faith and perseverance in the face of adversity kept me going. Victor Kasica, the oldest of my brothers, inspired me with his own formidable work ethic and determination to carry on when things got tough.

I also want to acknowledge my healthcare team, who eased my pain and made it possible to work on this book even when it was only one page at a time. Much gratitude goes to my excellent physicians: Michael Daras, MD, PhD; Ekong B. Ekong, MD; Lyall Gorenstein, MD; Winston Kwa, MD; Kaiyu Ma, MD, PhD; Tal Ronen, MD; Samir Sodha, MD; Daniel Tomlinson, MD; and Nelson Wong, MD. I also wish to recognize: James Romano, DC, the best chiropractor around; the wonderful therapists at Access Physical Therapy and Wellness, especially Jennifer Orphal, Deborah Larsen, and Kathy Coleman; the Pain Whisperer, Tom Chi; and the woman with the magic hands,

Connie Wehmeyer at Subtle Energies Holistic Health Center.

Thanks also to my legal team—Eva Panchynshyn, Edie Adams, and Scott Goldstein, and their very capable staff at Ouimette, Goldstein and Andrews, PC. I would not have made it without you.

Many people offered assistance as early readers, editors, and critics, including members of the Hudson Valley Romance Writers of America, most notably Liz Matis, Allie Boniface, Yolanda Sly Kozuha, Kat Attalla, Janet Lane Walters, Wendy Marcus, and Maureen Morrison. Writers need each other. Thanks for your comments and suggestions. I would be remiss if I did not mention editor extraordinaire Bobbie Christmas at Zebra Communications, whose book "Write in Style" is my writing bible, and who's advice I've sought and gained many times although we've never personally met.

Family members also took the time to read the manuscript: my mom, my mother-in-law Eleanor Sciucco, and my sister-in-law, Jane Sciucco. I so appreciate your support.

My former case management colleagues at Orange Regional Medical Center read the first finished version of this novel and filled me with hope that one day I'd hold it in my hands as a published book: Lisa Enright, Sue Ann Kalin, Annette Cort, and our data analyst Barbara Kwiecinski. I miss you guys.

Marianne Sciucco

Much appreciation goes to Mike and Connie Wehmeyer for proofreading and editing the final manuscript.

Several other friends reminded me that I had a book to write by asking me how it was coming, and without their gentle prodding, I may have sat on the project indefinitely. Thanks to Mike and Genevieve Haines and Bret Guaraldi for pushing me forward.

Most importantly, I'm grateful to the many people with Alzheimer's disease and their loved ones who passed through my life during my tenure as a hospital nurse and case manager. You taught me so much.

In addition, above all others, I thank my loving Lord and savior Jesus Christ, *from whom all good things come.*

About the Author

I've wanted to be a writer ever since I learned such a person exists. I love words and stories. I studied the craft of writing as an English major at the University of Massachusetts at Boston and worked for a time as a newspaper writer. I later became a nurse. In 2002, I put the two together and began writing about the intricate lives of people struggling with health and family issues. When not writing I work as a school nurse in a community college in New York's Mid-Hudson Valley, where I live with my husband, Lou, and daughter, Allison. To follow me, please visit:

MarianneSciucco.blogspot.com

@MarianneSciucco on Twitter

Marianne Sciucco

   Marianne Sciucco fan page on Facebook

   Marianne Sciucco on Google+

Sign up for my newsletter "Marianne Sciucco's Adventures in Publishing" at:

MarianneSciucco.blogspot.com

and I will send you a free PDF of my short story "Ino's Love," previously published in *Kaleidoscope and now available on Kindle.*

I read and respond to all my email. Please drop me a line at:

MarianneSciucco@gmail.com

How you can help
end Alzheimer's disease

If you are concerned about Alzheimer's or have a family member with the disease, consider joining the Alzheimer's Prevention Registry.

Created by Banner Alzheimer's Institute (BAI) and its community and scientific partners, The Alzheimer's Prevention Registry consists of people who are passionate about combating the disease. They see Alzheimer's as a very significant health issue for the nation and believe more must be done to stop it—starting right now.

By joining the Registry, members commit to helping end Alzheimer's without losing another generation. They step forward and protect their own health or that of loved ones and friends. In turn, the Registry allows them to be part of an online community that provides them with regular updates on the latest scientific advances and news, information on overall brain health and potential opportunities to participate in prevention studies.

Signing up is quick and easy, so do it today at

registry.endalznow.org

The Registry is open to anyone 18 and older in the U.S. Turn your worries over Alzheimer's into advocacy and action.

Author Request

If you enjoyed this book, please be so kind as to post a review. Your support and comments really do matter and I read all reviews so I can get your feedback. It's simple: just go to my Amazon page:

amazon.com/author/mariannesciucco

and select "Blue Hydrangeas." Scroll down to where it says "Customer Reviews," click on the box that says "Write a Review," and start writing!

Thanks again for your support.

Marianne Sciucco

Made in the USA
Middletown, DE
28 July 2017